ALIEN LOVE

ALIEN LOVE

Stan Schatt

ALIEN LOVE

DOUBLE DRAGON

Prologue

A few students stared at the black limo navigating the narrow campus streets as it headed toward the Physics building. The old man's lips formed a slight smile that could have been a grimace. Retired astronauts, particularly those who had walked on the Moon, enjoyed plenty of perks. All they had to do is play by the rules. Astronauts' wives never complained publicly about the danger their husbands faced or the media's intrusion into their private lives. Astronauts never spoke off the record, revealed top-secret information, or complained about suffocating rules and regulations. Besides a nice pension, they enjoyed the best healthcare in the world.

Maybe that particular perk wasn't so great after all. A retired technician might succumb to cancer after a few months and die peacefully in his sleep, but a retired astronaut might linger for a year, thanks to drugs costing thousands of dollars. Well, maybe there was a reason God wanted Major Frank Buchanan to stick around a bit longer. While he had been brought up believing that he always should do the right thing, he had gone along to get along for much too many years. His hand brushed against a thick manila folder in his jacket pocket, and he saw that his driver was staring at him.

"You sure you're up for this, boss?" The worry lines on the driver's normally placid face reflected his mounting concern.

"I'll be fine, Jimmy. If I could make it to the Moon and back, I can make it to the fourth floor with the help of a damned elevator."

Few students looked up from their phones to watch as Buchanan slowly climbed out of the limo. Of course, if they'd known who he was, they might have paid more attention. His face had been plastered on cereal boxes as well as on every TV set on the planet. He reached into his pocket for a pain pill and swallowed it without water and then leaned heavily on his cane as he walked slowly into the physics building and found the elevator.

A middle-aged man wearing a tweed jacket responded to the soft knock and motioned for the former astronaut to take a seat at a table surrounded by bookcases overflowing with books on astrophysics. He carefully locked the door before joining his guest.

"So, it's true? They lied all those years and called me every name in the book; I was right after all."

Buchanan's craggy face broke into a small smile. "Yeah, you almost fucked up everything. I'm surprised someone hasn't taken you out by now."

"I was sorry to hear about your...condition."

"You ought to be happy. I probably wouldn't be here if I had months left and not days. It's hard to believe I'm one of the last rocket jockeys still alive who've left this planet and returned in one piece. Maybe I've been around too long."

"Have you brought any documents with you? I'm particularly interested in those memos from NASA that you mentioned as well as that report analyzing Moon images from the probes."

Buchanan reached into a coat pocket and pulled out a thick folder. "If I were you, I'd make copies of this stuff and then hide them where they'll be safe.

I'm not joking when I say people have died for knowing just a fraction of what's here."

The professor's hand shook as he took the envelope. He stared at it for a couple of minutes without speaking and then reached for a video camera that was on a bookshelf. "You said you wanted me to record what you have to say?"

Buchanan nodded. "Nobody's going to believe you no matter how great a reputation you might have. You'll need a video to prove you didn't cook up this story on your own. Even with the video, I'm sure NASA is going to say that I was on meds and hallucinating and not in my right mind."

"I agree. That's why I asked you for copies of some of those internal memos as well as some of the photos that showed up missing when I put through my Freedom of Information request."

"I've given you enough ammunition here to make some of those hotshots shit bricks. Promise me you'll be careful. You can't trust anyone. I'm convinced a couple of my buddies are dead because they reached the point where they were fed up and ready to talk."

Professor Aaron Starling pressed the record button on his video camera as the former astronaut began to speak.

"It started long before we went into space. I know you've heard about the flying saucer that crashed in Roswell, but let me tell you how that led to the formation of a group known as Majestic-12 and how they've managed to keep a lid on everything. I'm not proud of the fact that my fellow astronauts and I let them muzzle us. You worry about your family and your reputation when you're young. I'm too old now to worry about those things. I outlived my only child, and I don't have much time left myself."

Buchanan felt his strength waning, but he forced himself to go on as long as he could. He popped another pain pill and grunted his appreciation when the professor helped him up. He saw now that he hadn't noticed that the office's walls were covered with star charts including a large poster that read WE ARE NOT ALONE. He smiled and nodded before staggering toward the elevator. He knew he'd be sick that night, but he always completed his missions. He saw Jimmy talking on his cell phone. When the driver spotted him, he quickly hung up and headed in his direction to give him a hand.

On the way home Buchanan looked at Jimmy's taut face. "Is everything okay? Did you have a fight with your girlfriend?"

Jimmy bit his lip before replying. "Nah, I just found out that my landlord's going to raise my rent."

"Can I give you some dough to tide you over? I'm sure the good ole USA isn't paying you that much to drive an old man to his doctor appointments."

"I'll be okay. It's been a real honor driving you, sir." "I'm not dead yet," Buchanan reminded him. "Not yet," the driver muttered to himself.

Chapter 1

The bearded man with his head covered in the traditional manner smiled and waved a greeting as he drew closer to the SEAL team. Jack recognized him and started to relax, but then he saw a dark shadow radiating from the figure and realized what was about to happen. He shouted for his men to move back and began firing his weapon just as the suicide bomber's belt crammed with explosives blew up. All was quiet then except for the sounds of the dying and wounded until the whining sound of a siren grew louder. Only then did Jack become aware of the sharp pain in his hip and that he lay face down on a dusty street in Afghanistan near the border with Pakistan.

Jack Starling's broad chest glistened with sweat as he forced himself awake. He shook his head like a dog shaking off water after a swim. The SEAL recruiting poster on the wall reassured him this was his room and not the Valley of Death or even the hospital in Kabul. He slowed his heart rate by meditating until he felt himself gain control, and then he picked up the pad of paper and pen on his nightstand and dutifully recorded the nightmare beside the date. Doctor Wilson always asked for his log before giving him a prescription to refill the pills that occupied a prominent place on his kitchen counter. He ignored the jackhammer in his head and lay face down on the floor.

Jack counted out his one hundred pushups and three hundred sit-ups. He added some clapping pushups until his body finally felt loosened up. The full force of the hot water messaging his scalp while he showered finally eased his headache. He dutifully took his Paxil along with a couple of Aspirin and studied himself in the mirror. He wondered what Mom and Dad thought when they saw him. *Definitely not a chip off the old block, that's for sure.* He looked about as much like them as a Rottweiler resembled a Chihuahua. Tony, his SEAL team leader, called him Ivan Drago after the heavily muscled blond Russian boxer in the *Rocky IV* movie because he knew Jack hated that comparison. Okay, he admitted that he looked like the chiseled actor who played Drago, but he wasn't a damned Russian. A SEAL shouldn't have to prove that he's an American through and through to anyone. After what he went through over there, he didn't owe civilians anything; in fact, at the very least they owed him a fair shot at a job. He glanced at the suit he'd worn to yesterday's interview. It now lay lifeless on the floor where he'd stripped it off the minute he came home. *How many times do I have to listen to bloodless wimps tell me I'm not quite right for a job or even worse, overqualified because of my leadership experience?* He remembered now what that pompous overweight asshole had said while looking over his resume. "We don't need trained killers to manage our Navy contracts."

He hadn't had much of an appetite in months, so he contented himself with finishing the remaining coffee in the pot and then taking out his lighter and lighting a cigarette. *Breakfast of champions*, he thought and smiled as his eyes caught the triton image on the lighter. He considered that his good luck charm. How else could anyone explain how he survived the traitor's attack?

Even though Jack now received a monthly disability check, he spent most of his time job-hunting by knocking on the doors of San Diego contractors who did business with the Navy. Today would be different, though. He put on a fresh shirt and jeans and picked up the scrap of paper containing the address of the coffee shop where Pete Moon wanted to meet him. The bright midmorning sunlight surprised him until he realized that he'd lost several hours because he'd finally fallen back asleep after turning off his alarm. He studied his apartment's parking lot and looked for suspicious looking passengers seated inside any of the parked cars before stepping away from the door. That's one lesson Afghanistan had taught him.

The Starbucks off Governor and the 805 was empty except for several student squatters who occupied tables within power cord distance of the few electrical outlets. Apple laptops or iPads and oversized coffee cups competed for space on their small tabletops. He glanced at them and wondered if he had ever looked that young and clueless as a college student.

His eyes passed over a man sitting with his back against a wall, and then they returned and studied him before he decided that must be Pete. The men of SEAL Team Five had been like brothers until the day their world exploded, yet Jack barely recognized the man who looked middle-aged. Although he couldn't be a day over twenty-five, Moon's salt and pepper colored hair now displayed far more salt than pepper. The dark circles under his

11

eyes and the way they flitted left to right and back again made him look like a cornered raccoon. He noticed a much darker than usual red glow around his friend as he rose and embraced him. Their hug lasted long enough that some people turned and stared until they self-consciously took their seats.

"I feel rotten that I didn't get over to the hospital to visit you. I really meant to do it," Moon said.

"Forget it. You were there when it counted." "Is anyone from our unit still over there?" Jack shook his head. "I heard they even forced Dixon out, and I always figured him for a lifer." "I know you've got your own problems, but I have to talk to someone." Moon spoke with far more hoarseness than Jack remembered.

He didn't respond immediately but watched as the small figure wiped the perspiration from his forehead with a frayed handkerchief even though the room's air conditioning had caused some of the students to don sweaters.

"Time is one thing I have plenty of right now since no one wants to hire me."

"Give me a break. You came out on top at your father's college. You'll find something. I'm hoping with all your smarts, you'll know what I should do."

"What's all the mystery? You wouldn't tell me anything over the phone."

Moon stood suddenly and almost overturned his chair. "Just a second. I'll be right back."

He brushed past Jack and hurried out the door. He thrust one hand in his pants pocket and kept it there while he did a slow one hundred- eighty-degree turn and studied everyone he saw. Apparently satisfied, he returned and took his seat.

"Are you expecting someone?"

"No, I'm just making sure we're alone. Remember how you always warned everyone about Ahmed? You did that eye squinting thing and saw a black cloud around him."

"Yeah, I remember. A lot of good that did."

"None of us blame you. Look around and tell me if you see anything unusual, one of those bad colors you used to look for when you questioned the ragheads."

Jack surveyed everyone in the room and then shook his head. "Everyone's cool. You were the only one who believed me about the color thing."

Moon shrugged. "That's because you never fingered the wrong guy. What I'm going to tell you sounds like some kind of science fiction movie. I just want you to hear me out. I'm cold sober. I haven't had a drink in weeks."

"Now you're starting to scare me."

Moon's jaw tightened. "You damned well should be scared. Do you remember Matthews? He left about a year before all the shit hit the fan."

"Sure, he always led us with a stick up his ass and insisted on following every rule in the book, but at least you could depend on him to do his job. He would have been okay if he didn't kiss up to Tony every chance he got."

"I ran into him right after the brass ran us out. He knew all about it, but it didn't bother him none that we wouldn't turn on you. He offered me a job."

So? That's good, right?"

"I thought so. He worked for a contractor that some government agency hired to do top-secret security work, and I had the clearance. It seemed like pretty easy money for the work, so I took it."

Jack let his breath out slowly. "Okay."

"Just let me tell it my way even if it takes a while. We were assigned to a unit stationed in New Mexico near the border with Colorado."

"Not much there. I'm guessing your job was to keep tourists away from an airbase."

Moon smiled for the first time. "That's what I figured, but it didn't work out that way. You ever heard of a secret base in New Mexico?"

Jack shook his head

"What I'm going to tell you is above top-secret. Our government's been lying to us for over fifty years. It's working with aliens who are conducting experiments on us."

"Oh come on! I don't know what you've been drinking or snorting, but that's just bullshit. You've seen too many *X Files* reruns."

Jack started to stand, but Moon grabbed his arm and pulled him back into his seat. His hand shook.

"Just hear me out, and then you can decide whether or not to help me. You owe me that."

Jack glanced at his watch and then shrugged. "We'll do it your way. I've got an appointment with my shrink in a couple of hours, so I don't have all day. Let's hear it."

Moon paused and eyed Jack before continuing. "I'm part of this unit, mostly ex-SEALs and Rangers, so I'm feeling pretty good that we can handle anything, you understand?"

"Sure."

14

"We fly into this small airfield, and everywhere I look I see guards locked and loaded. Our leader takes us to the side of the mountain where there's a huge elevator big enough to hold a truck. We go down for a long time, so long that I'm thinking maybe it was broken and we are going to crash. Jesus, I'm thinking, this damned thing might never stop. When it finally does stop, we see soldiers wearing uniforms that I don't recognize. These guys are huge, and they're built like you except with dark hair and brown eyes."

Jack sighed again. He looked at his watch, but Moon continued his story at the same pace.

"Suddenly I'm on my own because I make a wrong turn. That doesn't bother me none. I figure I'd take a shortcut and catch up before anyone notices. The passageways down there aren't marked. I look through a window and I see a room with a woman inside. She has tubes running out of her mouth, and it looks like she's sleeping. That's when I see them."

"You're going to tell me you saw aliens, right?"

"I turn the corner and I see the biggest, ugliest thing I've ever seen. It sees me and presses something on its belt, and suddenly it looks like one of us."

"Maybe you just imagined it."

"I act on instinct and start shooting. Suddenly it's a freaking monster again and bleeding green goop. Two others that look like soldiers wearing the same type of uniform turn the corner and begin firing at me. I hit the ground and roll around the corner, and we have ourselves a firefight. The rest of my guys find me, and all hell breaks loose. With

15

all the shooting, my guys begin to see dead aliens, and that freaks them out."

"They saw the monsters too?"

"Yeah, Matthews himself shows up a few minutes later and tells us to retreat. We make it back to the elevator and out of the tunnel. Meanwhile, he tells us not to say a word because we really didn't see anything. It's all a hallucination."

"I've heard that one before."

"Yeah, but this time the brass put us in separate rooms and questioned us for hours. This doctor told us that we were victims of hallucinations caused by an experimental biochemical weapon. He said that they would have to reassign all of us since we're now susceptible. Then this guy wearing a black suit and smelling like he's CIA came into our room. He stared at us like we were lower than shit and said that the weapon is top secret, and the good ole USA would lock us up and throw away the key if we ever said anything."

"But you knew you really did see something?"

"Yeah, so on the way back home I got this vibe that something's not right. You know the feeling. Matthews went from being all buddy- buddy on the way there to avoiding me and not looking at me on the way home. I went to my apartment, but I couldn't shake that feeling. So I waited until dark and then I climbed out my back window and checked into a dump of a motel where I could pay cash with no questions asked. The next morning I turned on the news and found out that my apartment was gone, blown higher than a kite. The reporter said I must have left the gas on, and that's what caused the explosion. You know me well enough to know that I never use the oven. If you can't fry it or nuke it, you don't want to eat it."

"And you know it's too much of a coincidence, right?"

"I know they're after me. I need a place I can stay for a little while until I figure things out."

Jack glanced at his watch. "Sure, stay with me. It's not much of a place, but you should be safe. There's still plenty of time for me to run you over there now. You can relax, maybe take a shower, while I go visit my shrink."

The two men left the Starbucks and drove toward the freeway ramp. A black sedan left the parking lot and then began skillfully following several car lengths behind.

Chapter 2

Jack drove toward his apartment, but stole a glance at Pete and saw him staring at the side mirror. When his friend sighed and visibly relaxed, he concluded that a suspicious car must have turned down a side street. Jack worried his friend might be paranoid.

"No suitcase?"

"I'm traveling light. I won't be with you very long. I just need a day or two, and then I'll move on."

"Do you need any cash?"

"Thanks, but I cleared out all my accounts yesterday. I'm not taking any credit cards with me either."

"No wheels?"

"Too easy to trace me. I'll probably take a bus."

"Where are you going?"

"It's better if you don't know. I just need to keep my head down low for a while until they forget about me. I wish I could get over my nightmares."

"You're not the only one with nightmares."

Just like old times, Jack thought as he unlocked his apartment's door and they entered cautiously. It's so easy to fall back into a routine, he thought as the two men moved slowly from room to room. They entered each room much the same way they had moved through houses in Kandahar Province. Once they had given each room a thorough examination, Jack brewed a pot of coffee and insisted Pete take it easy while he kept an appointment with his shrink.

The modern medical office building with sunlight reflecting off its metal and glass exterior could just as well be the headquarters of some technology company. It was a far cry from the dingy VA Hospital that referred most of Doctor Felicity Wilson's patients. Jack studied the other people in the waiting room, but thankfully he didn't recognize anyone. Even though he looked normal, he knew he wasn't right inside. All the patients in the waiting room were defective products the Navy sent back for repair. Unlike other Navy equipment though, the shrinks couldn't fix him by simply tightening a screw or replacing a battery.

The young physician assistant called his name and led him to a small room with two chairs and a table containing pamphlets that addressed a variety of stress-related conditions. A faded picture on a wall showed a man wearing an Army officer's uniform.

Doctor Wilson brushed the red bangs out of her eyes and asked her usual set of questions. Nightmares? Headaches? Panic attacks whenever anything seemed out of the ordinary? Jack gave his usual responses while observing that she never hurried him and seemed to hang on every word he said.

"I'd like you to try to take some of the visualization exercises we've been practicing a step further now. Just before you go to sleep, think hard about how you could change the nightmare to give it a better ending. It's not easy, but it will help you move past this bump in the road that's keeping you from recovering."

"Better ending? Don't you think I've thought about that? If I ignored Tony's orders and blew away Ahmed the day before he attacked us, I would have saved two members of my team; unfortunately, the Navy would have convicted me of murder. You'd have one less patient, and we wouldn't be having this conversation now."

"What about well before the attack? Isn't there anything else you could have said to convince Lieutenant Franklin to listen to you and not to Tony?"

"Based on what? If I told him that I disobeyed direct orders because someone projected the wrong colors in his aura, he would have locked me up in the loony bin long before Ahmed blew himself up."

"We're not going to have the conversation about colors and auras again. I don't believe in that stuff or in astrology." Jack detected an unusual note of exasperation because usually she had a lot of patience with him.

"I can't help what I see. By the way, you're pink, just in case you're wondering."

"I'm going to assume pink is good. As far as your visualization, just use your imagination. Let's say that you found proof that Ahmed was a double agent and showed the proof to Lieutenant Franklin."

Jack shook his head slowly. "You've never been in the service. Part of the SEALS' code that we live by is that we never go over a superior's head. I did that. I did it for the right reasons, but I did it."

"But you were right, and your commanding officer was wrong."

"Not if you read the official report. Franklin and my team leader closed ranks and covered themselves. It was my word against theirs."

"What about your men?"

"What about them?"

"Didn't they back you up?"

"Sure, that's why they're all civilians again. I appreciate everything you're trying to do for me, but I've thought about nothing else but this for months now. I can't think of anything I could have done differently. I *know* I did the right thing."

"You mean when the attack came?"

"Yeah, then and before."

"But you blacked out."

"I saw the results when I snapped out of it. My team told me what I did, and I believe them and not the brass."

"You must have done something right. They awarded you all those medals."

"Didn't you ever hear of 'blood money'? Every time I look at those worthless pieces of metal I think of how different things would be if someone believed me before the traitor decided to pull the pin."

Doctor Wilson continued questioning him and jotting down notes as he answered. Finally she glanced at her watch and sighed.

"We'll have to pick this up again at our next session. I'll call in a refill to your pharmacy. Just try some of those visualization exercises and use your imagination. You're a good man, Jack. You need to stop beating yourself up. Eventually, you'll realize you have nothing to feel guilty about."

She rose and shook his hand before pulling him closer and gently patting his back a couple of times before releasing him. Doctor Wilson had to be close to his mother's age, but no one ever accused Marjorie Starling of being nurturing. Jack started for the door and then realized that he saw a resemblance between the Army officer in the picture and his psychologist.

"Your father?"

"Yes."

He waited, but Doctor Wilson didn't speak although he noticed her eyes glisten. He turned and left, closing the door softly behind him. Jack thought of Doctor Wilson on his drive home. She had called him at home after one traumatic session to ask if he were feeling better. No other physician had ever done that. He'd give her suggestions a try even though he knew they wouldn't work. Pete, Ricky, Bill, and all the others were alive, and that's what counted. He'd just have to live with what happened to Hank and Joe. He saw their images in his dreams every night. When he thought about Pete, he remembered their conversation that morning. Nothing ever shook up that little guy because he never worried about things the way most people did. He never read a newspaper or a book, and certainly not any science fiction. In fact, for a minute Jack wondered whether his friend could even read. Once he confided that he'd joined the service so he could finally have a decent pair of shoes and a winter coat. He'd downed the Navy chow as if it were in a gourmet restaurant. He never spoke about government conspiracies, black helicopters, or expressed views on anything related to politics. He just did his job until something scared him bad enough to push him over the edge. *Maybe the military really did invent some kind of biological weapon. That made a lot more sense than anything Pete said,* Jack thought as he drove home.

Pete had stood up for him at the hearing, and now he would help his buddy any way he could. *Maybe Doctor Wilson could treat him,* Jack mused as he parked in his usual spot in front of his apartment. He pulled out his key as he reached the door and decided to make some noise so that he wouldn't startle his friend. Pete was probably armed and jumpy enough to take a shot at him if he surprised him. He turned the key back and forth several times before opening the door.

"Pete?"

No one answered, and he saw that his coffee table had been tipped over. Jack stood stock still for a few moments and listened very intently. He heard someone's TV blasting a commercial for Geico Insurance but otherwise nothing but silence. He had learned to rely on his ears when searching homes in Afghanistan, so he stopped occasionally to listen as he headed toward his bedroom. His heart pounded when he saw his sheets on the floor and a red stain on the wall near his light switch. The small table near his bed now lay shoved against the closet door. He moved cautiously, checking the bathroom and then the kitchen, but those rooms looked undisturbed except for a damp towel hanging over the shower door.

Jack went back into the bedroom, forced open the sliding closet door that had come off its tracks, and reached all the way to the left until he found his

23

old raincoat that had a tear in the lining on the inner side of one pocket. The tear created a secret compartment inside the lining. He put his hand into one of the deep pockets and then into the lining and pulled out his Sig Sauer along with three extra magazines. He always kept the gun loaded. Jack knew his friend could take care of himself, and he had a sudden thought that chilled him. *How many men had it taken to overpower him? Some people must have followed us back to the apartment. Whoever they were, they probably were watching me right now.*

Jack double-bolted his door that night. He placed his gun under his pillow in exactly the same way as he did on those many nights when he slept in hostile territory.

Chapter 3

Jack woke the next morning to a banging on his door. He grabbed his gun and walked to the door, as the knocking grew louder and more insistent. He opened the shade slightly and saw a solitary hulking figure. Upon closer inspection, he noticed that the man wore a uniform. Jack opened the door and then stared as he recognized the man.

"Scarpo, what the hell are you doing here?"

"We have to talk."

He spoke in the same low, rumbling voice that Jack had learned to hate. He noticed Scarpo now sported officer stripes.

"I've got nothing to say to you, and I'm not taking orders from anyone now."

"It's about your buddy Pete."

Jack stepped aside, but took his hand from behind his back so Scarpo could see the gun. Scarpo took a seat and carefully pulled up his trousers to maintain their crease. He pointedly ignored the weapon as if it were of little importance.

"What did you and your goons do to him?"

"I don't know what you're talking about. We had a report that you were seen talking to him."

"That's bullshit. Is this about what he saw in New Mexico?"

Scarpo's eyes widened and the muscles in his jaw tightened. "I wouldn't believe anything he told you. He's been buttonholing everyone he knows and telling some half-ass story. I'm here to tell you that it would be much healthier for you to forget anything he told you."

"What have you done with him? What exactly did he see?"

"Your buddy's turned to drugs since his release, and now he's spreading rumors. We don't have him. If we find him, we'll get him some help. You might put yourself in danger if you hang around him."

"Your concern is very touching, and I know just how much you care. You haven't forgotten about Karachi, have you?"

Scarpo's face tightened. "You won't get the chance to sucker punch me a second time."

"We both know it wasn't a sucker punch. If I find out that you have Pete, your buddies won't be able to save you this time."

Scarpo's face darkened, and he snarled, "I just came here to give you some friendly advice. I thought with your disability and all, you might have trouble understanding what's really happening. When we settle our accounts, I won't need any help. You're not getting lucky twice."

He rose slowly and glared at Jack before turning his back as he headed to the door. He walked slowly and calmly as if he controlled the situation and then slammed the door behind him.

Jack felt dizzy; his heart pounded as if it would break right through his chest. He forced himself to sit down and concentrate on his mantra, even though his mind was going a hundred miles an hour. His body slowly returned to normal. He rose too quickly and felt a wave of dizziness and nausea. He steadied himself and walked to the door and double locked it while looking through the peephole to make sure Scarpo was no longer around.

He glanced at his watch and then headed toward the bathroom. He would meet his mother for lunch and then call in some favors to learn where Scarpo worked and whether or not he stashed Pete there. Once he knew for sure, he'd reassemble his old team and rescue him. *Never leave anyone behind* he thought and remembered how often that message had been drummed into his head.

***

Parking at noon in downtown San Diego is always a nightmare. Jack found a spot on an isolated part of Ash Street, so that meant walking several blocks to the fashionable Gaslamp Quarter where his mother had made a lunch reservation at Fernando's. He readied himself for the inevitable stares and worried expressions from women who would go out of their way to avoid him. He consciously tried to steer clear of approaching women who were walking alone, since he knew from past experience that his size frightened them. Sometimes a woman walking in his direction would spot him and then deliberately cross over to the other side of the street before he could step aside.

He understood a solitary woman's unease when faced with someone his size, but he resented the fact they judged him without knowing him. He felt like shouting, "I'm safe. I've never hurt anyone who didn't have a gun. Why can't you understand that?" Instead of saying anything, he just made sure he gave solitary women plenty of space and tried not to make eye contact.

Jack covered the distance to the restaurant rapidly and saw his mother at a corner table where she was in the process of downing a large margarita.

It reassured him to see the pale yellow light radiating around the well-dressed middle-aged woman. Her aura displayed different colors when she became angry or sad, so he knew even before she spoke that today she felt fine.

Most people never thought of Marjorie Starling as short or overweight because of her commanding presence. When she spoke in her courtroom voice, waiters stood a little straighter and moved much faster. She closed her law office when she first brought Jack home and did not go back to work until he started high school. Now she ran a booming practice that catered to parentless couples seeking in vitro fertilization by providing surrogate mothers to carry their babies to term along with all the legal adoption paperwork. She held up a basket of chips and motioned for him to come over and join her. She stood and they embraced. Her strong arms tightened around his back. She held fast to him until he started to feel uncomfortable and pulled away.

She seemed a little unsteady on her feet, but Jack chalked that up to the margarita. Unlike his father, she usually came across as calm and unemotional. He remembered he had asked her advice once when he was still in high school; she had responding by laying out the pros and cons of each possible course of action until he shouted, "I'm not your client. Just tell me what you think I should do."

They ordered their favorites. Marjorie had established the ritual of a biweekly lunch at Fernando's shortly after the hospital released him. She studied her son with her shrewd eyes before speaking.

28

"Are you taking your meds?"

"Yeah, I'm not sure how much good they do, but I take them."

"How's your hip?"

"Back to full motion. I'm jogging again."

"Are you sleeping any better? Tell me the truth."

"It's starting to improve."

"Well, the doctors said it would take a while. Have you talked to your father lately?"

"You know the answer to that."

"He misses you because he loves you so much. I don't understand why the two of you can't have a nice conversation without fighting."

"He's not going to change. How's he doing?"

"Something's bothering him. He used to sleep like a log, but now he's up pacing half the night."

"Are they still trying to drum him out of his department because he keeps writing that NASA is lying about little green men?"

"Don't make fun of your father. To answer your question, the administration cooled any plans it might have had to get rid of him when the Anderson Foundation gave him that very well endowed tenured chair. Still, he seems genuinely frightened about something. He's very secretive about some of the calls he gets at home, and he comes home late several times a week."

"You don't think...?"

"Of course not. I'd trust Aaron if he were the only man on an island filled with women. I know you're not being serious, but I don't even want to joke about that. You and he always used to be so close. Maybe you could drop by his office."

"He's still talking about me going back to school, isn't he?"

"Yes, I won't lie to you, but I just don't understand why you can't get past that."

"Mom, you know I love Dad. I just can't go through another argument with him over what I should do with my life. I'm not strong enough to deal with all that emotional stuff."

"You're probably right, but I'd love to see you both in the same room without any shouting."

Jack shrugged. They'd had this conversation too many times already.

"Have you thought about grad school now that you're out? With your grades, your father says you're guaranteed a fellowship."

"I'm not ready. You sound like him now."

"Let's change the subject."

"Were you able to find out any more about my birth parents?"

"Things were much more secretive back when you were born. Don't give up. I have someone working on it right now, and I'm hoping I'll have something for you very soon."

"Thanks, Mom. It would really mean a lot to me. You'll always be my mother, but I just want to know what they were like."

"I understand because I run into this at work all the time. Your father doesn't understand why you're rejecting him for someone who never raised you. I've tried reasoning with him, but he's very emotional when it comes to that subject."

The food arrived, and they both ate silently for a while. Marjorie reached over and put one hand on her son's arm. She opened her purse with her other hand and placed a check on the table near Jack's plate.

"Take this to help with your expenses until you can get back on your feet. If you won't take it as a gift, take it as a loan."

Jack felt his face redden; he hesitated, and then reluctantly put the check in his wallet and thanked her. He turned away so she couldn't see the expression on his face.

"Have you started dating again? Twenty-five is too young to live like a hermit."

"The only people I've met lately have been at the hospital, and they're more screwed up than I am. When I meet someone special, you'll be the first to know."

"I'd like to have a grandchild before I'm too old to enjoy it."

Marjorie sighed as she looked at her watch and then signaled emphatically for the waiter to bring the check. When it came, she studied it as if it were a court document before placing two twenty-dollar bills on the tray. "I have to get back to the office. If you don't want to call me at home, reach me on my cell. I worry about you."

The two embraced, and then Jack watched his mother barrel her way through some tourists who were blocking the exit. He took two of the candies from the tray and put them in his pocket as he rose and headed back to where he had parked his car. The sidewalk was crowded with tourists radiating all the colors of the rainbow. A man radiating a black shadow hurried past him while avoiding making eye contact. He watched the man until he was out of sight before his heart slowed to normal.

Jack started to relax as he passed A Street with its bumper-to- bumper one-way traffic and turned on to Ash where it was almost deserted. He caught sight of his car a couple of blocks ahead as well as a woman about a half block ahead of him. He couldn't see her face, but she was a real knockout if her blond hair and figure were any indication. He picked up his pace slightly when he realized she reminded him of Suzie and began daydreaming about her and about the time when everything had been great between them.

Suddenly a dark gray van sped past him and pulled up beside the blond. A door opened and a hulking figure jumped out and began grappling with the woman who, surprisingly, seemed to be holding her own. The man wrapped one hand around her mouth to keep her from screaming and tightened his grip around her with his other arm as she continued to struggle. As Jack drew closer, he noticed a bulge in the attacker's pocket that he assumed was a weapon. The man released his hand on the woman's mouth and delivered a forearm to the side of her head that stunned her into submission. He started dragging her toward the van.

Everything slowed down for Jack except his heart, and that speeded up. He took in the distance between them, the fact the van had moved slightly ahead of the couple, and the lack of any other bystanders. He began running and quickly drew alongside. It felt good to feel healthy again. When he played linebacker at El Camino High, his coach taught him how to bring a ball carrier down. "Follow through on the tackle," he had lectured and often demonstrated. Jack crashed into the man and knocked him to the sidewalk. The woman collapsed on the ground. When the assailant began to pull some kind of weapon out of his pocket, Jack grabbed the large man's arm and felt his strength.

They battled for control of the weapon. Jack could feel the man gaining leverage on him, and he realized that he had to win that battle before the accomplice joined them. He rarely fought anyone who could match his strength, but this man's arms felt like steel. His SEAL instructor had told him while training him in hand-to-hand combat, "There are no Marquis of Queensbury rules when you're trying to survive. Use any vulnerability, and don't worry about fighting fair."

Jack slammed his elbow into the man's groin, but there was no reaction. *How the hell could he not feel that?* Jack thought. Desperate now, he kneed the man's stomach and felt the fight go out of him. Jack grabbed the weapon. It was small and shaped like a gun, but it had a button rather than a trigger. The barrel hadn't been hollowed out. *Why was the man carrying some kind of toy around with him?* The man suddenly lunged at Jack. Instinct and training kicked in as he aimed the weapon and pressed the button. He began to feel a little dizzy, but he saw the man fall to the ground as blood seeped out of his shoulder. The van backed up and the passenger door flew open. The attacker struggled to his feet, lunged toward the van and staggered inside as it accelerated accompanied by screeching tires.

Jack looked at the blood on the ground. He'd seen too much blood in Afghanistan, including the stained ground where the traitor's bomb went off.

Still, none of those bloody puddles were as thick as what was on the sidewalk. As he studied the puddle, he thought, *the blood must have mixed with some oil on the road. Why risk getting shot or arrested to try to kidnap someone in broad daylight downtown?* He heard a low moan and turned in that direction.

Chapter 4

The woman lay flat on her back on the sidewalk and groaned as Jack studied her. He didn't see any bleeding, but she might be suffering from internal injuries. He debated whether or not to call 911. *Would the police assume he did this?* Her blond hair piled high on her head reminded him of murals he had seen in history books that depicted upper class Roman women. Her high cheekbones and generous mouth balanced a small nose, but an ugly purple bruise covering one cheek ruined what otherwise would have been perfection. She opened her eyes as he bent over her. When she saw him, her eyes opened even wider.

"Gliese," she said in a weak voice.

"I'm not sure what language you're speaking. Do you speak English? My name is Jack, and I'm going to take you to a hospital because you might have a concussion."

The woman shook her head. "No, don't take me to the hospital. *Please*."

"I'll take you home then. Where do you live?" The woman's eyes closed and she lay still. Jack became aware of her shallow but regular breathing. He reached down and placed his hand on her carotid artery and smiled in relief. She was alive and seemed coherent, wherever she was from. Her English sounded perfect, but somehow it didn't quite ring true because it seemed too perfect. He couldn't place her accent, although it reminded him of the way some of the Afghan guides spoke, at least the better-educated ones who had visited the states. He decided to take her to his apartment

35

where he could administer first aid. He lifted her easily and, placing one arm under her arm, he half-carried her to his car, placed her in the front seat, and then carefully buckled her seatbelt while his mind flashed to how difficult it would be to explain her unconsciousness and her bruise if a cop pulled him over. The last thing he needed in his life right now was to be accused of assaulting a woman he didn't even know.

Jack carefully observed all the traffic laws on his way home. He kept mouthing the word she had spoken, *Ga leese*. It had a musical sound, but what did it mean? Why did she look at him so strangely, as if he were some kind of ghost? Cars honked and passed him, but he didn't care. He glanced at the woman several times, but her eyes remained closed. Her breathing seemed to deepen, though, and his SEAL training told him that was a good sign. He pulled into his apartment complex parking lot. Once again, he placed one of his arms under her arm and maneuvered her toward his apartment, breathing a sigh of relief when he didn't see anyone watching them.

Jack held her with one arm as he reached the door while using his other hand to find his keys. His hand brushed against the strange weapon, and he realized that its toy-like size had caused him to forget that it still lay buried in his pocket. He opened the door and carefully placed the woman on his sofa before rushing back to the door to double-lock it.

Jack studied her face and saw that she remained beautiful despite her ugly purple bruise. Suddenly she opened her eyes and stared at him as she struggled to sit up. Recognition flooded her eyes.

"Do you remember your name?"

"Cassandra. You're Jack? Thank you for what you did." Her voice was soft and musical.

"Who were they? What did they want with you?"

"I ... don't know. Tell me who you are."

"There's not much to tell. I was a Navy SEAL. Now I'm just another guy looking for a job."

"A seal?"

Jack laughed when he saw the confusion on Cassandra's face and explained.

"So, you are good at killing people?"

"Just people who want to hurt our country. When you first saw me, you said something. It sounded like *ga leese*. What did you mean by that?"

She didn't reply immediately, but studied his face first. "I... was confused. You reminded me of someone else."

"If you feel up to standing, I'll give you a ride back to your home."

"Please, could I just rest here awhile?"

"Sure." Jack took one of the blankets off his bed and bent down to wrap the blanket around her. Cassandra lifted a hand and tentatively touched his shoulder, moving down to his biceps and pressing her fingers into the muscle. She seemed totally absorbed.

"Are you sure you feel okay?"

Rather than answering his question, she responded with several questions of her own. "Do you live here alone?"

"Yes."

"Do you have any children?"

Jack smiled. "I don't even have a girlfriend."

"How old are you?"

"Twenty-five."

Jack started to ask Cassandra her age, but then he bit his tongue. He'd been in the SEALs and away from women far too long to feel comfortable talking to one, especially one so beautiful. He felt her eyes studying him.

"Tell me again what a SEAL does." Despite her soft voice, the request sounded more like a command and Jack complied. He told himself that he just wanted to keep her talking because she needed to stay awake as long as possible in case she had a concussion. Still, part of him realized that he just wanted an excuse to be near her.

"What about you? What do you do for a living?"

"I'm ...a scientist; there's nothing exciting about what I do. You would find it boring. What does a SEAL study in school?"

Jack hesitated and then told her the truth since he had chosen a major far different than anyone he knew in the service. Anxious to keep her interest, he described his college classes. She questioned him about some of his advanced math courses.

"And you were number one in your class? That's very impressive."

"I feel like you just gave me a test. Did I pass?" Jack tried making his question sound like a joke, but he realized just how little he knew about her. She had managed to deflect every question with one of her own.

Cassandra's deep blue eyes seemed guileless. "I just wanted to know more about the man who saved my life."

"I don't know anything about you."

"There is not much to tell. I studied biology in school, and now the work I do is very technical and boring. Could we talk later? I need to close my eyes for a little while."

Jack studied the beautiful face marred by that purple bruise that seemed to grow larger as he watched. Her slow rhythmic breathing convinced him that she had fallen asleep almost immediately. He went to his room and closed the door softly. He crept into the kitchen later and fixed himself dinner while Cassandra slept through the noise. When he checked on her before going to bed, she lay still and apparently hadn't moved in hours.

When Jack awoke, he threw on some clothes and hurried into the living room and found it deserted. Cassandra had folded his blanket very neatly and left it on the sofa. He searched the rest of his apartment, but she hadn't left a note. He flung the door open and surveyed the parking lot but saw no sign of her. *Where could she have gone without a car?* Jack asked himself. Part of him worried that he imagined the whole thing, but he felt the smooth touch of the toy-like weapon when he reached into his pants pocket and sighed. He'd never see her again; they weren't even in the same league.

Chapter 5

Jack sat in a sports bar in Coronado a few days after meeting Cassandra and realized that watching the tables filled with people enjoying their lunches made him feel even more alone. When he saw a blond at the other end of the bar, he studied her more closely because from a distance she resembled the woman he had rescued. *Cassandra. What a knockout but way out of my league! She'll never call or come over, and I don't know where she lives,* he thought. He looked at his watch and wondered if Maurice would show up. He decided to give him another half hour because traffic out of the base at lunchtime could be miserable.

The TV on the wall was showing a Padre game. He didn't bother to look at the score because he didn't care, even though two greybeards at a table behind him were watching every pitch and second-guessing the manager. Only diehards rooted for a team that never won. He glanced at the table to his right and noticed two men about his age clad in almost identical dark suits with expensive looking ties; they sat across from each other talking on their cell phones. At another table two ramrod straight men with gray short-cropped hair sat on high stools while they nursed their drinks. *They must be ex-Navy officers enjoying their retirement in paradise,* Jack mused.

The network suddenly interrupted its broadcast of the game, and Jack saw Frank Buchanan's very recognizable face on the large screen. He read the text crawl below the picture and noted that the famous astronaut had died of a heart attack. *Another one of the good guys is gone*, he thought as he remembered the time their paths had crossed when the astronaut had spoken at his college; later he had joined the legend along with his father for lunch. He imagined his father would be devastated at the loss of one of his personal heroes.

A rail thin black man with a receding hairline entered and studied the customers before heading for Jack's table. He paused and glanced around the room once again before sitting down.

"Man, I shouldn't be here. You are trouble with a capital T."

Jack smiled. "I'm happy to see you too, Maurice; I'm not going to get you in trouble."

Maurice wasn't smiling. "Too late for that. I'm here, but I can't stay long. If anyone sees me talking with you, words going to get back to the base. I don't need that kind of trouble."

"I appreciate you coming. I won't keep you long. I just need some information because I'm out of the loop now."

"You bet your ass you're out of the loop. You're damned lucky they didn't hang you by your balls for what you done."

"I saved my team and that's all that counts."

"Fat lot of good that done. They out in the street just like you."

"They're alive."

"I give you that." Maurice looked around once more before speaking. "Most folks including me think you done the right thing by your boys. It's just the system that's screwed up, and ain't nobody going to fix it. Tony and his boy gonna keep kissing ass until they both make Admiral."

41

"I need a little help."

Maurice nodded. "That's why I'm here. You just name it."

"I need to find out who Mike Scarpo works for now and what duty station he calls home. I think he's locked Pete up somewhere, and I want to find out where so I can break him out."

Maurice's eyes widened. "That's crazy talk. You're talking about twenty years of hard labor, if they don't shoot you first."

"Let me worry about that. I can probably get my shrink to testify I didn't take my meds and didn't know what I was doing."

"The word is that Scarpo is with some special unit. He got himself transferred after you left. I'll try to find out where he calls home, but I have to be careful. I got myself a wife and kid now."

"Don't do anything risky. Just see what you can find out. I really appreciate you coming. I guess I know who my friends are now."

Maurice stood up. "I can't promise exactly when, but I'll text you and set up a meeting if I hear something. Give me a few days. One of my buddies will be returning later this week from some special assignment in New Mexico."

Jack stood and they shook hands very solemnly. Jack took his time finishing his drink after Maurice left, ordered some appetizers, and thought about what he should do next. There was no sense in getting his team together until he knew where Scarpo worked and if he really had Pete. *Hang in there, Pete,* he thought. He'd settle up with Scarpo the next time they met.

Jack climbed into his car and drove across the bridge as he headed home. He monitored his rearview mirror and side mirrors and thought he saw a black sedan following him. He pulled onto the 163 and monitored the car now two cars behind him. Suddenly he changed lanes and swerved onto the 805. He wasn't surprised to see the black sedan following him.

Jack remembered he'd left his Sig Sauer in its usual hiding place in his raincoat. *Fat good that did him now!* He didn't trust the toy-like weapon in his pocket even though it did plenty of damage to the man who attacked Cassandra. He didn't panic, though, because his training kicked in as he began developing a plan. The freeway traffic moved smoothly despite the narrowing of lanes with the convergence of the 5 and 805. He knew whoever was following him wouldn't try anything until he exited to a less heavily traveled road. Jack grew up in San Diego and attended college there, so he had a clear mental map of the major streets. He searched his mind for what he needed.

He exited in Carlsbad at Palomar Airport road and headed east toward San Marcos. He knew this road had been designed by Carlsbad city planners to carry most of the commerce heading inland and that large delivery trucks and vans routinely used it. He knew that his vintage Pontiac Fury with flames painted near the headlights had plenty of power, so he moved to the far left lane and floored his gas pedal. The car shot forward. When he saw the black sedan speed up and move directly behind him, he realized that the driver was skilled enough to keep up with him.

Jack timed it so he would pass Aviara Parkway just as the light turned red. The black sedan drove right through the red light without pausing as several cars honked at it. *I shouldn't expect him to follow the rules of the road when he's trying to kill me,* he thought and then smiled to himself as he anticipated his next move. He saw a left turn lane ahead and calculated the speed of oncoming traffic. It was going to be too close for comfort.

He slowed only slightly as he moved into the left turn lane and then executed a U-turn so quickly that his tires screeched. Hearing the frenzied honking and sensing the approaching traffic, he floored the accelerator and felt his car explode forward. He looked in his rearview mirror and saw the black sedan begin a U-turn just as a large produce delivery truck approached. As Jack anticipated, the truck traveled much too fast for its brakes to slow in time. The black sedan made a sickening crunching sound as it slammed into the median, bounced off, and tried to straighten its wheels just as a motorcycle cop put on his flashing lights and came up beside it.

Jack smiled and kept driving. The cop no doubt called in the license plate of the sedan, so it wouldn't do the driver any good to shoot the officer. Right now the driver only faced reckless driving charges. In all likelihood he would flash a special ID card resulting in his release after a single phone call. His smile faded as Jack suddenly had a thought that made his blood run cold. *Scarpo must have someone following him.*

Jack drove home and settled in for the night. He watched a rerun of an old game on the NFL channel, but he couldn't give the game his full attention because his mind focused too much on Scarpo and Pete. He wondered if the black sedan's driver was in jail or spying on him from somewhere in the parking lot. His gut warned that trouble was coming, so he retrieved his gun and stuffed it in his pocket.

He shut off the television around ten that night and started to head to his bedroom when someone knocked on his door. It wasn't Scarpo's "take no prisoner's" kind of knock. He heard three short gentle knocks, as if someone were apologetic for coming so late. He pulled aside the curtains and his jaw dropped when he recognized the figure. He quickly opened the door.

"Can I come in?" Cassandra said.

"Sure," Jack said and stepped aside to let her pass. He bolted the door behind her, but she didn't seem surprised by his action.

She wore a dark green blouse that hung tightly across her chest. Her eyes reflected that color and made them look green. Her jeans hugged her hips. Jack couldn't see her aura, but he realized the bright lighting in the living room obscured it. In any event, there were no black shadows to worry about. The purple bruise still discolored one side of her face and made her look vulnerable. Jack desired to put his arms around her and protect her. She walked through the living room, picking up objects occasionally and examining them and then continued through the kitchen and before stopping to glance into the bathroom. Jack followed her, completely puzzled by her actions. She continued on to the bedroom before stopping and turning to him.

"This is your bedroom." She said it as a statement and not as a question, but Jack nodded anyway. She turned to him and lifted her head so she was looking directly in his eyes.

"I am very grateful that you saved me." She spoke so softly that he had to strain to hear her.

"You've already thanked me. We're square. I just happened to be there at the right time. I'm sure anyone would have done the same."

"No, that's not true. I want to thank you in a very special way."

Jack started to object, but Cassandra pulled her blouse over her head. She did it quickly and efficiently without any artistry or flirtatiousness, far more like someone stripping for a physical exam than a pole dancer trying to entice her audience. Her hands fumbled as she unhooked and removed her bra. Her breasts were flawless. Jack saw her erect nipples and felt himself stirring but couldn't get one thought out of his mind. *It's been such a long time. I wonder if everything down there still works.*

Cassandra proceeded to kick off her shoes and pull off her slacks. Clad only in her panties now, she began to pull Jack's shirt over his head as he helped her. She stared at his chest, mesmerized.

"I've never seen such muscles."

Jack pulled off his pants and felt his penis press hard against his shorts. He removed them and then lifted Cassandra and carried her to the bed. He pulled off her panties in one motion. Her body was smooth as glass without even a trace of hair, not even any fuzz on her arms. Jack noted the lack of any pubic hair and wondered just how painful waxing must have been. He marveled at her perfectly round belly button along with her perfect breasts.

Jack kissed her hard and dug his lips into hers. At first she didn't respond. In fact, she started to pull away from him, but then almost immediately she moved closer and returned his kisses. He shoved his tongue down her mouth, and it rattled her enough so that she pulled her face away. *Okay, I better take this slowly and gently* Jack thought as he began to kiss her neck and heard her breathing quicken. He rubbed his hand across one of her breasts and began caressing her nipples. She gasped again and moaned. He felt himself pulse as her excitement fueled his own.

He forced himself to slow down because he wanted to make their first time perfect. He used his hands and tongue on her, and then he placed his hand on her clit and softly massaged it until he felt she was ready.

"I've got condoms in the drawer. Hold up just a second while I unwrap one," Jack said.

He started to reach for the drawer, but Cassandra put her hand on his arm to restrain him. "Everything will be fine. I want to feel you inside."

Jack turned and balanced himself on his elbows, but he ran into a wall as he tried to enter her. He paused, puzzled.

"Is something wrong?"

She's a virgin. Why the hell didn't she tell me? She wants me to continue, though. Jack thrust himself down as hard as he could and felt something give. Suddenly he was inside her.

47

Cassandra gasped.

"It should feel better soon." Jack shifted both of them on to their sides so that his weight would not be on her.

He began moving rhythmically. At first Cassandra did not respond, and then her hips started moving as well. Jack began to move his hips faster. He felt a slight tremble, and then he felt Cassandra's body responding. She was trembling now. Suddenly she screamed, and he felt her orgasm. Her reaction caused him to explode inside her. Time seemed to slow down. He held her as Cassandra tried to catch her breath.

Jack kissed her deeply and put his arms around her, drawing her more closely to him. She was perfect. He felt like his senses were tuned to a much higher level than ever before, yet he couldn't detect her scent despite her perspiration. He ran his fingers through her hair, and he felt her respond to his touch with another orgasm. He moved a hand slowly down her body, marveling at the smoothness everywhere, including her thighs.

"Are you sure you don't have any kids?" Cassandra asked softly.

The words startled Jack. "I told you I didn't have any children. If I'm a father, I'd sure as hell know it."

"But you are capable of being a father...aren't you?"

Jack flushed. "Yeah, I guess. Why are you asking me those questions?"

"I feel different. Maybe I'm pregnant," Cassandra said softly. Jack sat up and felt cold sweat run down his back.

"Jesus. I thought you had some protection. You didn't say anything."

"I'm just being silly because it's much too soon to know."

Jack just stared at her and thought, *I win the lottery, and she turns out to be crazy. Why talk about babies? What are the odds of a baby if you only do it once?*

"Tell me about your parents," Cassandra said. "What?" "I just want to know more about you now that we've had sex."

She seemed oblivious to Jack's reaction. "It might be better if you called it 'making love.' When I realized you were a virgin, I should have stopped. That first time should be special. It should be with someone you've known for a while. We don't even know each other."

"We know each other now. I thought you liked me. Are you saying we shouldn't have *made love*?" The phrase sounded odd the way Cassandra said it.

"Of course I like you, and you're a woman who can decide what she wants to do with her body. It's been great and everything, but I think you need to go home now," Jack said and thought, *God, I've never kicked anyone out of my bed. I can't believe what I'm doing, but she's nuttier than a fruitcake. Maybe I'll wake up and find I just dreamed this. That would make more sense.*

"Did I say something wrong?"

"I don't know why you want to get pregnant, but I'm not the guy for that. I'm asking you to please go." He rolled off the bed and started to put on his clothes.

49

Cassandra watched him for a couple of minutes. Then she rose and showed no embarrassment, as she stood there naked. She paused and then and began dressing as well. Neither spoke. Finally she walked to the door, unbolted it and left without saying a word. Jack looked through the window and watched her disappear. He bolted the door once again and sat down in his favorite chair.

His mind was racing. *I doubt I'll ever get to sleep tonight. How could someone that hot and willing still be a virgin? Why does she talk the way she does? Why did she make me feel like I'm just a piece of meat?*

Chapter 6

Jack woke to bright sunlight streaming into his room. He reached for his notepad, and checked off the "No Nightmare" column while noting that he didn't have a headache. He whistled for the first time in months as he washed, dressed quickly, and made some coffee. He couldn't get Cassandra out of his mind. *Why do the most beautiful ones have to be crazy?* He hungered for her even though he knew she spelled trouble. Gradually his thoughts turned to Pete. He glanced at his bookshelf, noticed his high school yearbook, and suddenly he realized John McCray was the perfect person to help him, assuming his old friend wasn't locked up in some loony bin.

He checked his watch. If he hurried, he could reach El Camino High in time to catch Mrs. Rollins between classes. He knew that the woman considered her lunch hour inviolate, and she wouldn't respond to any students knocking on the door to the teacher's lounge during that time.

Jack parked in a loading zone because students occupied all the legal parking spaces. As he jogged across the campus, he remembered what it had felt like to be a BMOC. He still remembered the game with the Oceanside Pirates and how Suzie looked in her cheerleader outfit. He signed the register in the Principal's office and put on a visitor's badge and smiled when he recognized the trophy case in the corner as well as the trophy for winning the California Division II championship. His team had gone undefeated.

He followed a path that led past the cafeteria and noticed that the grass needed cutting. Someone had painted over graffiti on the wall, but the shadow was still visible. He reached the math and science wing and turned in the direction of Room 101. Mrs. Rollins never changed rooms.

He visited her during a vacation break from college many years ago, and she told him that she intended to keep her room until she retired or they had to carry her out feet first. He arrived just as the lunch bell sounded. Students poured out of the room. He realized some things never change as he identified the gangbangers, the nerds, the jocks, and even a few preppies as they hurried past him without giving him a second look. He glanced in and saw Mrs. Rollins shaking her head emphatically while she corrected an equation a student had written on the board.

Finally the student left and Mrs. Rollins gathered her bag and stuffed in her book and papers. She started for the door but stopped when she saw Jack.

"Jack, is that really you?"

"Yes, ma'am. It's great seeing you again."

Mrs. Rollins wore her gray hair in a tight bun. Everything about her reflected her preference for efficiency over show. She frowned and pursed her lips before continuing. "I remember reading something about you leaving the Navy. I forget the details, but it sounded messy. Are you all right?"

"I'm fine now. I wanted to ask you about someone in my class."

"Sure, I try to keep up with as many of my gang as I can, especially the ones who took calculus with me. I'm so proud of you, valedictorian with a math major! I still use you as an example."

"College math was a snap after your classes. I wondered if you still kept in touch with John McCray."

"You mean Hawk?"

Jack smiled. He hadn't heard that nickname for years. McCray's beak and small eyes did make him look like a hawk. Still, he never met anyone smarter when it came to science and math.

"I lost track of him. Didn't he go to Cal Tech?"

Mrs. Rollins nodded her head sadly. "He's the only student I ever taught who went to Cal Tech. He graduated with honors in math and physics. Can you imagine? He came back here when his father passed away and took over his business."

"You mean the mortuary?"

"Yes, he visited me once, and I told him to hire someone and go into science. He's much too brilliant to waste his talents as an undertaker."

"I don't want to keep you from lunch any longer. I need to talk with him about something." Mrs. Rollins blue eyes still shone brightly. Her hand gripped Jack's arm and he felt her strength. "Did you ever marry Suzie? You seemed like the perfect couple."

Jack realized he'd clenched his jaw and tried to relax it. "No, we just couldn't agree on some things. I haven't seen her in years. She probably has five kids by now."

Mrs. Rollins still held his arm tightly. "I hear she never married. She came back after college and works for Zynx. She still comes over here to see me occasionally. You ought to say hello."

Jack freed his arm. "I'll come back and we can talk when we both have more time. It's great seeing you again." He hugged the small woman and then headed to the door. He looked back and saw the teacher remove a tissue from her purse and dab her eyes.

He thought about Suzie. If she hadn't agreed with Dad, then maybe they might have had a life together. She never understood that. He still remembered their last conversation when he told her he'd joined the Navy right after college graduation and intended to become a SEAL.

Jack took El Camino Real to Cannon Road and then turned down the road leading to the McCray Mortuary. As he pulled into the parking lot, he noticed only two cars, both parked in staff parking spots. As he entered the building he caught the faint odor of formaldehyde. That smell triggered memories of high school biology and, of course, frog dissection. Hawk had delighted in pulling pranks that would have gotten anyone else expelled. Once he had attached thin, almost invisible, wires to a frog already cut open for dissection. When the teacher neared the dissected creature, it suddenly began thrashing and making the most inhuman croaking sounds. Miss Harris had screamed and bolted from the room. Later Hawk explained to his friends how he sent electrical signals to nerves in the frog's legs and throat.

Jack hurried through the empty sales room and down the hall toward the double doors labeled NO ADMITTANCE where he expected to find McCray. When he pushed the doors open, they squeaked and then revealed a bulky figure hunched over a naked body while he applied makeup to the corpse's face. The mortician weighed at least twenty pounds more than in high school and wore his hair much shorter, but Hawk hadn't changed.

"Careful, he might not be dead. You have to watch out for the living dead," Jack said, mouthing the same words with the same grave tone that Hawk used several years earlier just before he sent the frog the electrical impulses that almost got him suspended.

Hawk turned and stared at Jack before circling around the body until he was close enough to embrace him.

"Jack, it's been forever! I read about the troubles you had with the Navy. I'm so glad to see you!"

"I'm glad to see you too. Mrs. Rollins told me where to find you."

"Yeah. I don't think she'll ever forgive me for not joining some tech company and making a zillion dollars when they went IPO. She wanted so much to brag about me."

"She still brags about you. I'm sorry to hear about your father."

"Thanks. I've given up trying to explain to people why I came back here. This job gives me time to think. I've probably read enough the past few years to earn a Ph.D. The difference is that I read what I'm interested in. This place is challenging to run, so I'm never bored."

"I guess you don't run into that many women, though, at least any still breathing."

Hawk smiled ruefully. "Well, there are plenty of grieving widows, but I guess you mean someone our age. You're right. I'm on Date-Match.com and have a few things going. What about you? I lost touch. Did you and Suzie ever marry? What are you doing now?"

Jack described his stint in rehab and his recent unsuccessful efforts to find a job. He watched Hawk nod as he continued to work on the body. His large hands moved with surprising dexterity to apply just the right amount of makeup.

"I know a lot of people. Maybe I could put a word in for you."

"Maybe. Do you have any time to talk? It's kind of important."

"Sure, if you don't mind standing around while I finish up Mr. Jackson. My bookkeeper is the only other person here, and she never comes back here because she's afraid of dead bodies."

"We can talk here."

"Put on one of those aprons hanging on the wall behind you. I don't want you complaining that I need to buy you a new shirt or pants."

Jack obeyed and watched his friend meticulously apply makeup to the corpse. Now he felt surer than ever that Hawk was the right person to answer his questions. He had always been the resident expert on science fiction who could tell you what theoretically could work in *Star Trek* and what was just fantasy.

Jack related Moon's story about a supposedly secret base in Dulce, New Mexico that housed aliens. He watched Hawk's face, but it didn't seem to register any surprise; instead, his friend nodded and smiled.

Hawk's hands stopped applying makeup to the body. He stared at Jack. "Hell, everyone knows about Dulce. Half the science fiction writers are obsessed with it. Are you telling me it's real?"

Jack took a deep breath and then repeated Moon's story about huge aliens who somehow were able to look human simply by touching some device on their belts as well as his friend's contention that the aliens were trading technology with the government.

Hawk was nodding enthusiastically now. "Sure, some people think we've been trading with aliens for years. The rumor is that's how we got our hands on semiconductor technology. Dulce is supposed to be where we house the aliens while they conduct their experiments."

"What experiments?"

Hawk winced as if to make it clear it wasn't his idea. "From what I've read, they're trying to create hybrids from humans and aliens."

"My friend says he saw a woman that must have been part of some kind of experiment."

"Christ! That's right out of the *X Files*. I can't believe you're telling me it's real!"

"You can't repeat any of this. The military told him he hallucinated because of a biological weapon he ingested and that he never really saw any aliens. What I want to know from you is if his story makes any sense."

Hawk placed one hand on his chin and rubbed it. Jack remembered now that Hawk always did that when he did any serious thinking.

"Yeah, I've read all kinds of accounts by people our government labeled as crazy. There are just too many reports out there to ignore. Science fiction writers have taken some of these anecdotal stories and turned them into some great novels. I think Dulce is real."

"Tell me what you know."

Hawk always had a photographic mind. He described the Draconians as a reptilian race that used small gray aliens known as the "Grays" or "Travelers" as their assistants. He stopped almost in mid- sentence and slapped his forehead like one of The Three Stooges.

"I'm so stupid. I have a better idea. In ten minutes I'll be done and then and I'll show you what I have on Dulce."

Jack's mind was spinning. *Reptilian aliens? It sounded like science fiction. Pete's story is too fantastic to be real, but if Hawk says it's possible...* The time seemed to take forever. Finally Hawk nodded and placed the body back in cold storage. He led Jack out a back door to a ranch style house on the other side of a wide expanse of grass.

"You live here? It must be nice to have such a short commute."

Hawk shrugged and motioned for Jack to follow him inside. They walked through a modest sized dining room into a snug study lined on all sides with floor to ceiling bookcases overflowing with books.

He moved a ladder to a corner and climbed several steps so he could reach the higher shelves. His hand hovered over several books before pulling three of them and stacking them on the top of the ladder. After spending a few more moments

58

searching for other books on the subject, he climbed down the ladder and blew dust off the books.

Hawk placed the books down on a side table before picking up one and combing through it. He stopped and then nodded before describing the author as someone who supposedly worked security at Dulce. He turned to a page and showed Jack a diagram revealing seven levels buried deep below the ground.

"What the map doesn't tell you is that he says everyone traveling below level two needs to have a special card with their name, accurate weight and security clearance. If anyone tries to take an elevator down without proper security clearance, all hell breaks out and armed guards and aliens appear and start shooting."

Jack whistled and stared at the book. "Could I borrow it?"

"Sure, here are a couple of more books that fill in some of the details." Hawk then described rules apparently negotiated by the Draconians so that only they were permitted to carry weapons on the lower levels where the aliens worked on developing hybrids of humans and themselves.

"How big is the complex?"

Jack noticed that Hawk was breathing heavily now and speaking faster. He waved his hands in a broad motion. "That's the interesting part. Supposedly Dulce is connected via high-speed magnetic trams to other sites throughout the country. The authors claim that other countries have similar underground networks. Some entrances are relatively easy to find and not heavily guarded while the main entrances have ultra-high security."

"Why not guard every entrance?"

Hawk nodded and smiled as if he had anticipated Jack asking that very question. "The authors say that the government used natural terrain to cover some entrances. You'd need to know what you're looking for and maybe even have satellite photos to find some of these smaller entrances. I'm not sure what good it would do, though, because guards would probably shoot any trespasser on sight."

Jack's hand brushed against the small weapon in his pocket and reminded him of its presence. He asked hypothetically about the possibility of creating a weapon capable of blowing a hole through something like a laser but having the side effect of causing that a person to feel dizzy when it was fired.

Hawk always treated the most ridiculous science question with the upmost seriousness. He rested his hand on his chin and thought for a few seconds before finally replying. "If firing it made you feel dizzy and nauseated, it's probably some kind of high frequency weapon. Sure, very tightly directed frequencies at high enough ranges could have that kind of impact. Did your friend see a weapon like that?"

Jack paused before answering. "The guy with one was incredibly strong. I punched him in his nuts and he didn't even react."

Hawk smiled broadly and rubbed his hands together. "Maybe he wasn't human."

"Oh come on. Now you sound paranoid."

Hawk shook his head and wagged his finger at Jack as if he were a teacher explaining the most

60

basic of facts to the class dunce. "Reptiles don't have the same junk in their trunk that we have. Their reproductive organs are probably in their abdomen; I assume reptilian aliens would be built the same way. Did you happen to hit him in his stomach?"

"Yeah, that knocked the fight out of him."

Hawk put his hand on Jack's shoulder. "This is so cool! If you're thinking of going there, I'm in. I could help you with the science side of it."

Jack stared at his friend; his eyes focused on Hawk's ample stomach. "This will be a military operation and not a scientific expedition. The rule is that no SEAL leaves one of his own team behind. We have to bring back our brother no matter what. The best way you could help is to tell me anything you think will help us survive."

The friends talked for about an hour and then an ambulance delivered a body along with a rush order; apparently Mr. Terrell's family couldn't wait to get him into the ground. They agreed to meet again later that week.

Chapter 7

Jack found himself talking out loud as he read through the books Hawk loaned him. At one point he muttered, "Give me a break!" when he read about a woman claiming she spotted a reptilian creature in her backyard attempting to steal her pet poodle. Another man declared he had seen papers signed by President Truman that outlined a treaty with the aliens. A man claiming psychic abilities said he had seen several groups of aliens on Earth and that the planet served as a kind of Casablanca, a neutral planet currently at peace with everyone and a place where enemies mingled and spun their plots.

An article on yet another website described how NASA was lying to Americans about aliens on the moon and how photos sent back to earth had been doctored or declared missing to hide the incriminating images. The author described a mile long spaceship parked in full view of Earth's telescopes along with a huge pyramid structure that mirrored similar structures on Mars as well as in Egypt. He realized that his father's theories about the presence of extraterrestrial life paled in comparison with the elaborate claims of these true believers.

Jack shook his head and wondered at the number of lunatics out there and then used Google to learn more about some of the people quoted who claimed to have spent time at Dulce. A few had suffered fatal heart attacks while others who had been diagnosed as paranoid now resided in asylums. As far as he could determine, two former Army security officers just dropped off the grid entirely.

He thought about those two men. *Did government goons kill them? Were they hiding somewhere? Maybe they're locked up in some asylum.*

The video clips available online that claimed to reveal Dulce's secrets varied in quality. A few amateurish films depicted aliens that clearly were humans because of the cheesy looking homemade costumes they wore. In one poorly lit video, Jack could actually see the zippers of the costumes that the people masquerading as aliens wore. Those videos reminded him of some of the old *Star Trek* television episodes where the production team had run short of budget and apparently told the actors to put on rubber masks and pretend they were aliens. Jack labeled a few videos as possibly authentic; those clips made his blood run cold and scared him even though he didn't scare easily.

One notice on a website devoted to discussions about alien visitation caught his attention. A group calling itself Aliens Among Us met regularly at a coffee shop in San Diego. He made a mental note to attend the next scheduled meeting since it happened to be set for the following evening. The time passed quickly as Jack read firsthand accounts from people claiming to be former security officers who worked at Dulce. After several hours, he was so tired that he almost didn't hear a soft knocking at his door.

He looked through his door's peephole and hesitated. The knocking became more urgent. Finally he took a deep breath and let it out slowly before opening the door.

"What do you want?"

Cassandra faced him dressed this time in a red blouse that made her blond hair shine even more brightly. She wore the same tight hip- hugging jeans that accentuated her curves.

"That's not a very nice way to greet me. I just wanted to apologize for scaring you. I'm really not trying to get pregnant; I said it as a joke, but you took it wrong."

"You didn't scare me. I just think that we're not on the same page. I'm not interested in getting anyone pregnant because I have enough problems of my own without having to be responsible for a kid. I'm not sure you really were joking. You seemed damned serious to me. I'm sure you a very nice person, but maybe you should get some help. I know a good psychologist who might be just what you need."

Jack started to close the door, but Cassandra wedged her foot in and folded her arms defiantly.

"I didn't come here for you to get me pregnant. I just wanted to thank you for saving my life."

"I'm very happy I saved you, but you don't owe me anything."

"I just want to come in and talk," Cassandra said. Her soft voice and conciliatory tone caused him to reconsider. After hesitating a few seconds, he stepped aside and waved her in.

Cassandra took a seat in a faded armchair and crossed her legs demurely as if she were a guest at a high society tea party. She waited for Jack to take the seat facing her before continuing. Jack took his seat and felt defensive; he'd been rude to her. She seemed so small and defenseless. She made him feel like a skunk that had come to a tea party. Where were his manners?

He squinted at her but still couldn't make out her aura. He concluded that the light on the table beside her probably blotted it out. It made him realize how much he depended on reading auras when it came to evaluating people. Maybe he had used it as a crutch so long that now he felt clueless when it came to Cassandra. He squinted at her again in the hope that this time she'd radiate a color, any color. Hell, if she radiated black at least he'd know for sure his rudeness had not been out of line.

"Why are you looking at me like that?"

Jack hesitated and then shrugged. *What did it matter?* I'm sure you don't believe in auras and probably think I'm crazy, but usually I can see people's auras. I'm sure that makes no sense to a scientist like you."

"And what color aura do I have?" "I can't make it out. Maybe the lights are too bright."

"Have you always have been able to do this?" Cassandra's eyes focused on Jack like a laser beam as her voice rose.

"Yeah, but it's no big deal, and I don't want to talk about it. I'm sure that's not why you came."

"I really am grateful. I can tell you are a good person. I'm protected this time so you don't have to worry. I just thought that you would enjoy making love with me."

"I didn't say I didn't enjoy it. You're terrific. It's hard to explain. You don't know anything about me. Usually virgins know somebody pretty well before they give up their virginity. The first time should be special. Someday you'll probably be very angry that you lost your virginity to a perfect stranger."

Cassandra eyed Jack, apparently weighing her words before continuing. She spoke slowly and softly. He strained so he wouldn't miss any words.

"Most of my colleagues think it's just biology and nothing special or unusual, but they never have met you. The men I know are not special."

"You have a slight accent. Where do you come from?"

Cassandra shrugged. "Far away. You wouldn't know the place because it's too small to be on any maps. I'm happy we made love. You tried so hard to be gentle. Other men would have hurt me much more because they would only care about their own pleasure."

"I know it hurt, though. I'm not sure what you want from me. The few times we've talked, you always turned the conversation back to me. I don't know anything about you."

Cassandra smiled. "Scientists, particularly biologists like me, are usually rational and not emotional. We're really very boring people."

Jack couldn't help smiling. "There were a few moments when you were very emotional. I was afraid your screaming would bring the police."

Cassandra nodded, but she didn't seem embarrassed. "I never experienced anything like that. Do most women react that way when you make love to them?"

"That's not a question a gentleman would answer. I still am not sure what you want from me."

Cassandra smiled. "You make this much too complicated. Let me show my appreciation." She rose and headed to the bedroom without looking back.

Jack watched her, debated silently, and then rose and followed her. *The guys on my team would never believe this. They'd swear I made it up*, he thought. He remembered one summer in college when he'd taken the only job he could find, a door-to-door salesman. His middle-aged sales manager had smiled in a lascivious way and then spent an hour describing to him in detail how so many lonely women in lingerie had opened their doors to welcome him. Jack had nodded at the time but later shuddered at the thought of that man with his greasy hair and a belly that hung well over his waist hoisting himself on any woman. His team would assume he was no better than his old sales manager; they wouldn't believe a beautiful, sexy blond would knock on his door and throw herself at him. Part of him didn't believe it either.

He peeled off his clothes and joined the figure half-hidden under his sheets. She immediately flung herself on top of him and began kissing him. As Jack responded, he felt Cassandra's tongue in his mouth. *She hated this last time*, he thought. Her hands began to caress him in a way he'd only experienced once, and that was at the whorehouse with the worst reputation in Hong Kong. He felt himself grow hard. *She's picked up a few tricks. I can't believe it's the same woman. I feel like I'm with a pro*, he thought.

Cassandra's rapid breathing matched Jack's. They both climaxed and then Jack felt her hands touching him again. She repeated the process several more times and used her mouth very artfully until he lay totally spent. She began massaging his shoulders and back, and he felt himself begin to drift. Soon he slept.

Chapter 8

The sun streamed into the kitchen where Cassandra sat at the table. Jack poured her a second cup of coffee and then refilled his cup. He went to his refrigerator and removed an egg carton and began placing eggs on the counter. While Jack wasn't much of a cook, he could fry an egg with the best of them. He started to break an egg over a bowl when he saw Cassandra's expression.

"You don't want eggs for breakfast?"

"Could I just have some cold cereal instead? I'm a vegetarian."

"Sure." He compared Cassandra with Suzie who had loved a good steak. Maybe there was something to the health angle, though. Suzie always fought a grim battle to keep from gaining weight while Cassandra looked perfect. He brought the cereal and milk to the table and watched her eat for a couple of minutes before breaking the silence.

"Any plans today?"

Cassandra smiled. "I probably should go to work."

"Play hooky. It's too pretty a day to work."

"What do you have in mind?"

"Let's go to Balboa Park and spend the day. I bet you've never spent any time there."

"I don't get out much."

Jack studied Cassandra's face for a moment and then walked to the bathroom and collected a tube of sunblock. He tossed it to her. "I don't have a hat for you, so you better put some of this stuff on so you don't get a sunburn." Cassandra held the package up and turned it to read the directions. She smiled and began applying the cream.

He watched her and then handed her a towel so she could rub in the white spots. They drove toward the park without having to do much braking because they left well after the morning commuters and well before the lunch traffic. When Cassandra flinched at one point, Jack checked his side mirrors but didn't see anything until he heard a siren grow louder and closer. He saw an ambulance in his rearview mirror and quickly cut over to the far right lane.

"You must have good hearing."

Cassandra nodded and smiled. "I'm glad you don't have a dog whistle. That would really make me jump."

Jack found parking in an isolated lot on the museum side of the park. Construction on a new parking garage meant that many of the main parking lots were closed temporarily. They followed a path that led away from the museums until Jack veered off when he saw a grassy spot far away from the closest trees. He spread a blanket so they could lie in the sun. He couldn't stop staring at Cassandra because he never had seen anyone so beautiful.

She seemed oblivious to his staring as she lay there, smiling as the warm sunlight illuminated her face. She spread her arms as if she wanted to capture as much of it as she could.

"Is it cooler where you come from?"

Cassandra nodded. "No place is as perfect as San Diego. Did you ever have to fight in bright sunlight like this?"

"Once...and it went badly."

"What about when it's pitch dark? I'm interested in how you managed to coordinate an attack in the dark with infrared equipment. How did you do it?"

"I can't really talk about some of it. I'm surprised a biologist would want to know."

"I'm interested in anything that has to do with you. Just tell me what's permitted." Later Jack walked through the park with Cassandra while he held hands like a schoolboy on his first date. He led her to a cart where he bought them ice cream cones. She devoured hers and part of his. They ate pizza at a restaurant in the park and then Jack led her to a round shaped building labeled the Reuben Fleet Science Center.

"Why are we going here?"

"My surprise. Tonight's one of the nights when this museum has a planetarium show. My father used to take me, and they're actually pretty cool."

He paid for their tickets and found a seat in the auditorium. "What are we going to see?" Jack shrugged and looked sheepish. "I forgot to look, but they're always pretty good. I guess we'll both be surprised. If you don't like it, we'll just leave."

The room became pitch black as the ceiling suddenly displayed much too many stars to count and an actor's deep resonant voice boomed through the theater, "Are we alone? Will our search for intelligent life be successful?"

Jack saw that he'd been lucky because the screen had Cassandra's full attention. She leaned forward and whispered, "This is great."

The production showed pictures of the SETI project to find radio signals from intelligent life

71

forms. It then began to zero in on various star systems where there were planets in what was called the "Goldilocks Zone," the area where planets would not be too hot or too cold to sustain life. Jack soon found himself immersed in the show. The screen showed various candidates for life including some recently discovered planets such as Kepler-62e, Gliese 677 and 832c and Kepler-78f. Jack felt something ping inside his head, but he couldn't place it.

It was dark by the time the show ended, but a full moon hung low in the sky.

"Looks like we're going to have a full moon tonight."

Cassandra frowned and shuddered. "I don't know why there are so many romantic songs about that moon."

Jack smiled. "You sound like a scientist who just looks at it and sees a lifeless hunk of rock. I think that one reason there are so many romantic songs about it is that it's an easy rhyme. To be honest, I always liked moonless nights when we had to go into hostile territory."

Jack related a couple of stories that illustrated how the lack of moonlight saved his team. He held Cassandra's hand tightly as they walked back toward where he had parked. He thought about the movie they'd seen as he looked up at the stars.

"You'd think someone would send us a message. I seriously doubt we're alone in the universe."

"Why would they bother?"

"What do you mean? Haven't you seen Jodie Foster in *Contact*? Maybe the aliens could send plans for us to build a ship to visit them.

There's so much they could teach us about curing cancer and feeding everyone. Since they would have to be more advanced, they could teach us how to live in peace."

"Live in peace?"

"Sure, they must have something like the Federation of Planets in *Star Trek*."

"You make it sound so wonderful and peaceful."

"You don't think so?" Jack turned and studied her and saw that whatever he had said had changed her mood.

Cassandra's faced clouded. "Human history is filled with wars. Even Cro-Magnon man fought the Neanderthals. The winners write the history books. You're not going to find a book from the Neanderthal perspective about how to live peacefully. Aggression and the desire to preserve the race both seem built into all living things including insects."

"Maybe that's just because we're such a young planet. What does that have to do with an advanced civilization that has survived by learning to handle their conflicts by compromising and living in peace?"

Cassandra laughed. "I didn't want to turn this into a debate. I'm not sure why you think advanced alien civilizations have to be peaceful. What if an advanced alien race conquered everyone around them, so that other intelligent aliens didn't want to broadcast to alert them of their presence? I believe

Stephen Hawking said that we shouldn't alert aliens that we are here."

"So, when you think of aliens, you think *Independence Day* and not *ET?* That seems kind of cynical for a scientist."

"I'm just saying that real life might not be like a movie that ends happily in two hours with the humans defeating the horrible looking aliens. Maybe the aliens are more complicated than can be explained in a two-hour movie. Think about their appearance. The aliens in so many movies look alike—you know, short, gray with huge eyes. Look at all the variety we have on this planet when it comes to humans and birds and insects. Why assume the universe is so bland?"

"Okay, say you're right and the aliens come in all shapes and sizes. What would they want here? Our water and precious metals?"

"How would I know? Maybe different aliens want different things."

Jack smiled at Cassandra. "You mean they're not all here for our women?"

Cassandra stared at Jack with her mouth open in surprise. "What would they want with Earth's women?"

"I don't know. In most of the science fiction movies I've seen, it's the women that the aliens want to kidnap and take back with them."

Cassandra laughed. "Maybe that's because all the aliens in the movies were males."

They walked in silence for a while. The terrain looked very different at night despite the full moon. The friendly trees they saw that morning that promised welcoming shade now cast large shadows that could hide phantoms or real-life criminals. They heard breaking glass as they approached the parking lot.

"Wait here," Jack said and sprinted in the direction where the noise had come. He didn't look behind him, but he could hear Cassandra's breathing as she ran closely behind him. He started to tell her to stay put, but then he saw the two men standing beside his car. One held a crowbar that he had shoved through the driver's side window.

Jack ducked as the man swung the crowbar and then connected with an uppercut to the man's jaw that sent him sprawling. He heard a grunt and turned, expecting he'd seen the man's companion trying to attack him from behind.

Instead, he saw the second man lying flat on his back. Cassandra held her index finger against the man's neck. He appeared close to passing out.

"What did you do to him?" Jack said.

"It's just basic self-defense. I reacted when he attacked me. Do you need him conscious?"

"No, I don't want to have to wait here for the police."

Cassandra pressed her finger down more firmly and then released it. The man's body collapsed like a rag doll that had been thrown to the ground. Jack studied the man and marveled at Cassandra's skills. He placed his arms under one of the men's arms.

"I'll drag them over to the grass and then we'll leave. The police won't do anything to them even if we press charges. It's going to be their word against ours since there aren't any other witnesses."

Both men remained unconscious while Jack moved them so that they were partially hidden by a tree trunk. He swept the glass out of his car and covered the seats with the blanket they had used for sunbathing while trying to remember what kind of deductible he had on his insurance. He drove Cassandra back to his place while checking his rearview mirror to see whether anyone was following him.

Cassandra glanced at the books stacked in a pile as they entered the apartment. "What are you working on?" she asked as she looked at him with her guileless blue eyes.

"Just a trip I'm going to take with a few of my friends."

"Do you want company?"

"It's not that kind of trip. It's just a boring guy thing." They talked and eventually went to bed. Jack marveled how good they were together. Their bodies seemed to meld on their own as each anticipated what would please the other. Cassandra fell asleep in his arms. Soon he also was sleeping deeply.

Chapter 9

Jack slept until late morning; he stared at the empty pillow beside him. Cassandra's absence disappointed him because he still felt her warmth on the sheets, and that made him desire her even more. He vowed that next time he'd get her contact info before he let her leave the apartment. He showered and ate. He glanced at the stack of books Hawk had given him. Something didn't look right. He didn't remember leaving them in such a neat stack and thought he had left one book open to a specific page. He must have dreamed that. He shrugged and headed out the door.

As he approached the College Avenue exit, the freeway slowed as cars bunched up waiting to exit. He smiled as he thought about the lack of parking spots at San Diego State. All those people would be fighting over one or two vacant parking spots. His buddy Leroy called the parking stickers SDSU issued "hunting licenses." He just didn't have patience today with anything that slowed him down.

Eventually Jack made it to La Mesa and found a parking spot across from the Dallas Bar and Grill. He figured Maurice picked this spot because Navy people never drove that far from the base for lunch. He heard one of Johnny Cash's old tunes blaring over speakers as he entered through a side door and walked past several tables of business types wolfing down half-pound hamburgers and large pitchers of beer. Finally he found Maurice, almost invisible at a small table near the restrooms. He sat across from the man who looked even thinner and far more frightened than the last time they met.

"I almost didn't come."

"I can't thank you enough."

Maurice glanced around the room. Even though the loud country music drowned out conversation, he spoke in a soft voice. "Pete's in a bad way."

Jack's smile disappeared. "I saw the blood he left in my apartment. How bad?"

"At least a concussion. They used a concussion grenade and then tasered him, but it still took three guys to drag him out into the parking lot. He's in some place called Dulce now. Do you know where that is?"

Jack's blood drained from his face. After reading Hawk's books, he knew what Pete's odds for survival were. "Yeah, I really owe you."

"You sure as hell do, but both of us need to be alive for me to collect. I can't stay. I might already be in trouble for asking too many questions. Take care of yourself." Maurice laid a $10 bill on the table, downed the rest of his beer, and left. Jack sat lost in thought.

"Sir, I asked if your friend would be returning?" Jack glanced up as the young waitress's words finally registered. He shook his head and tried to clear it. Still dazed, he ordered a hamburger and watched the powerbrokers around him laughing and bragging about business deals. *I wonder what they'd do if I told them about the aliens? They'd probably have me committed*, he thought.

One man dressed in an expensive suit leaned over and whispered to a woman who resembled Suzie. Jack strained to look in order to make sure it wasn't his ex-girlfriend. He rose at one point and walked slowly past the couple toward the restroom.

78

He glanced at her and saw her face didn't measure up. Suzie had been a real beauty. *If only she hadn't tried to control me and mold me into someone I just wasn't. A guy should be able to set his own course and not be told what to do with his life.*

Now he realized just how empty he felt; he hungered for more than just a series of one-night stands. Cassandra excited him, but she was half nuts. Still, if she showed him she cared about him and not just his sperm, maybe they could build a real relationship, and she could get help for whatever problem she had. He went over that day at Balboa Park and smiled to himself. Lost in his thoughts, he drove in auto mode and didn't realize where he was until he exited the freeway.

Jack struggled to control his thoughts and turn them to another subject. *Stop feeling sorry for yourself. What about Pete? Focus on how you can rescue him.* He forced his mind to concentrate on a plan. He'd need to go over those books on Dulce again and reassemble his old team. *Would they be willing to put their lives on hold and take on what sounded like a suicide mission?*

He pulled into his apartment complex's parking lot and climbed the stairs slowly while he surveyed the parameter. He opened the door cautiously and sighed with relief when he sensed he was alone. Jack walked to his bedroom and pulled his gun along with some spare clips from his raincoat and placed them in a pocket. If the people who followed him ever forced him off the road and tried to grab him, he'd make them pay. He drove toward Front Street and parked near his mother's office. First he'd visit Fred and then he'd surprise her and see how her search for his biological mother was going.

Fred Goldstone's office commanded a view of the Coronado Bridge as well as the island. A thin woman wearing dark-framed glasses that hung at the tip of her nose ran her fingers though the gray hair she had wound into a tight bun. She looked up from her desk, eyed Jack, and didn't smile. "Do you have an appointment?" she said in such a way that she managed to convey her feeling that he didn't warrant an appointment.

"I'm an old friend. Please tell Fred that Jack Starling is here and it's important."

"He's extremely busy right now. Could you come back in a couple of hours?"

"I'm sure he'll be at lunch then and after that you'll tell me that he'll be tied up for the day. I'm not leaving. Buzz him and let him decide if he wants to talk to me. If he doesn't, I'll leave."

The woman hesitated and then shrugged. "His meeting should be over in five minutes. I'll ask him then."

Jack sat and picked up a *National Geographic* and found it had a special cover story on the SETI program. He smiled as he remembered the planetarium movie and then he turned to the article and began reading.

He thought about what Cassandra had said. Maybe people are lucky no aliens had heard our radio signals yet and responded. He focused on the article and then stopped, startled. There it was again, Gliese 677, one of the leading candidates for alien life. He remembered hearing it mentioned in the movie, but there was something else. He tried to

80

make the connection, but the receptionist interrupted him.

"Mister Goldstone has a few minutes. He'll see you right now."

Jack walked into the large office and Goldstone rose to shake his hand. Fred had left the Navy a couple of decades earlier and built a very large insurance practice, but he still served as a major source of support for his fellow SEALS, whether that meant helping them find jobs or helping them reconnect with friends. He seemed to know every current or former SEAL in the San Diego area. Jack carefully closed the door behind him before taking a seat.

"What's up?" While Goldstone's body no longer rippled with muscles, his gravelly voice and steel blue eyes commanded respect. His head seemed to spring directly from his body with no discernible neck. The man's huge hands looked as if they could still tear a man apart. While time had etched tracks across his forehead and under his eyes, his trim build suggested he still could fit into his service uniform.

"I need to talk with my former team, and I hoped you knew where I could find them."

"You guys sure got a raw deal. As I told you the last time we talked, you did the right thing and so did your men. They backed you even though it meant washing out."

"Thanks."

"I'm just surprised you guys haven't remained tight."

Jack flushed. "It wasn't my decision. I had my problems when I came home, and my shrink

81

ordered me to avoid seeing them for a while because of the nightmares I had."

"Why now?"

"I need to let them know what's happened to one of us. You know the motto about never leaving anyone behind."

Goldstone nodded and sighed. "Okay, I'll give you what I have." He turned to his computer and typed for a while and then printed a sheet. "Here's the contact info I have. I wouldn't be surprised if some of them would just as soon not hear from you."

"I argued with my shrink but she threatened to cut off my meds if I didn't follow her orders." Jack realized he was shouting and had drawn the attention of the receptionist, who crammed her neck to peer into the small glass portion of the door.

Goldstone spread his arms in a calming gesture. "I'm not the one you have to convince. I just meant I heard that some of them are having problems, and it's easy enough for them to second-guess the price they paid for supporting you."

Jack thanked him, took the printout, and left Goldstone's office. The receptionist made no effort to hide her unhappiness that he managed to break through her protective wall and see her boss. He walked down the block to his mother's office.

Her law offices occupied one of the top floors of the new high- rise and offered a view of the city that on a clear day extended as far as Jamul. The plump middle-aged woman sitting at the desk outside his mother's office eyed him and smiled.

"Jack, it's been too long. Is your mother expecting you?"

82

"It's nice to see you again, Mrs. Foster. No, I just thought I'd say hello if she's free."

She already had picked up her phone and whispered something into it. She listened for a couple of seconds and then nodded to Jack.

Marjorie Starling rose from her enormous desk and hugged her son as his feet sunk into the plush purple colored carpet she had insisted on for her office. "Is everything okay?"

"Everything's fine. I had a meeting down the block so I thought I'd drop by to say hello."

Marjorie Starling's face relaxed. "I meant to call you, but today's been one meeting after another. I just received verification from my investigator." She opened a drawer and withdrew a single sheet of paper from a file and handed it to her son.

"You found my biological parents?" Jack felt a lump in his throat.

"At least one of them. I'm sorry it took so long, and I hope it brings you some closure."

Jack's ears caught the inflection in his mother's voice. "Mom, you know better than anyone that this doesn't change anything. You'll always be my mother."

Marjorie bit her lip and smiled. "I go through this with so many clients; it's harder when it's your own child. I know how you feel. You need to do me a favor now." Her voice did not leave any room for a refusal.

"What do you need me to do?" Jack smiled. "Is there someone you want me to kill?"

"I hope it doesn't come to that. I told your father that we discovered at least one of your

83

biological parents, and he's taking it very hard. You need to go visit him right away. He has late afternoon office hours today even though students rarely come."

"Mom, you know where this is going to lead. It always ends the same way. I just don't have the energy to argue with him."

"I don't ask much of you, Jack, but I'm asking you as a personal favor to go there. He just needs some reassurance you love him. I know you do, but he needs to know it too. I love the man dearly, and I have to live with him. So, do it for me."

Jack let his breath out slowly. "I want to touch base with this person first, if I can. I've waited an awful long time. I'll stop by the campus right afterwards. He's there until six, isn't he?

Marjorie beamed at her son. "Yes, his undergrad class ends at four, and then he has office hours until six. He'll be very happy to see you. Just don't fight."

Jack smiled thinly. "I promise I'll try not to get in an argument with him. He probably has a fellowship already lined up and needs an answer tonight."

Marjorie put her hand on her son's arm and gripped it hard. "You're doing the right thing. I'm okay with you deciding on your own whether or not to go back to school. I can understand you want to do everything on your own terms. Just remember that your father loves you. Trying to help you is his way of showing that love."

She looked at her watch and sighed. I'm afraid I have a client scheduled in a couple of minutes, but we can talk later."

"I'll call you," Jack said. He failed to hide the excitement in his voice. He hugged his mother and hurried out of the office. Jack glanced at the paper his mother gave him. It identified his biological mother as Vivian White, age forty-one, currently a waitress at the Waffle House in El Cajon. Her California Driver's license listed an El Cajon address with an apartment number. Her age made Jack whistle. She had been only seventeen when she gave birth. *No wonder she put me up for adoption.* He called the Waffle House using the number his mother had given him.

"Waffle House," said a gruff male voice with a Spanish accent. "May I talk with Vivian White? I believe she's one of your waitresses." "She's off today. You call back tomorrow," the man said and then hung up. *That kind of charm will bring in the customers in droves,* Jack thought.

He plugged the residence address into his navigation system and headed to the freeway. Since he already was downtown, it would only be around a twenty-minute trip. He debated all the way there on how to start a conversation after twenty-five years. He realized that the bar where he met Maurice was only a few blocks from the woman's apartment. He'd been running in circles all day.

The El Real Apartments' best days had been several decades earlier. Now the faded green paint failed to hide the need for new stucco. The patched roof didn't inspire confidence that it could survive a major storm. Nobody had bothered to pick up the collection of empty beer cans that glittered on the faded lawn like fool's gold. Jack climbed to the second floor and knocked softly on the door. His heart beat so rapidly that he wondered if he would be able to go through with it. He heard a television blaring a commercial, and then he became aware that someone turned down the volume; he then heard footsteps inside approach the door.

"Who is it?" The woman's voice sounded tired as if she'd been sleeping.

"Mrs. White? Could I please talk with you? I've been looking for you for so many years."

Jack heard a deadbolt lock turn and a chain release before the door swung open. Time had not been entirely kind to his mother. Her blue eyes looked faded, perhaps from too many disappointments, while her light blond hair worn medium length now showed a lot of gray. Her high cheekbones and small nose suggested she once had been a real looker, but dark circles under her eyes and a forehead now filled with deep wrinkles reflected a life in which she struggled to survive.

She stared at Jack as if she'd seen a ghost. Her mouth began quivering and tears began rolling down her cheeks.

"I know who you are! You look just like John!"

Jack took a step toward the woman and tentatively reached out with his arms to hug her. She collapsed into his arms and sobbed. He noticed a man staring at them through his open door. "Maybe we should go inside and talk," he said.

Reluctantly the woman released him and opened the door wider. Jack entered and sat at a sofa facing an armchair. The woman moved the chair closer to the sofa and sat so that their knees almost touched. Stains of all kinds covered the gray threadbare carpeting. The room contained an uncomfortable looking sofa along with a small armchair and coffee table, a floor lamp with a bare light bulb that cast shadows, and an older model television turned to some soap opera that Jack didn't recognize.

"How did you find me?" she said in a shaky voice that revealed she hadn't regained full control of her emotions.

"There are investigators who do that for a living. I've been trying to find you for years. I hope I haven't upset you too much."

"No, but you have to understand that I was so young that I couldn't give you a good life by myself. John disappeared, and my parents refused to let me bring a baby home. I didn't have a choice. I loved you so much. I prayed every night you would have a good life."

Tears started to blur his vision. "I don't blame you. The people who adopted me gave me a good life. I graduated from college and joined the Navy. I became a SEAL. Can you tell me anything about my father?"

Vivian White took a few deep breaths that seemed to calm her. She opened the handbag on the adjacent coffee table and took out a few tissues. She dabbed the tears from her cheeks and blew her nose before she was ready to talk. "John looked exactly like you. He was so handsome and the smartest man I ever met."

"What did he do for a living?"

"He said he was a scientist, but he was very secretive. I never did find out where he worked. He spent lots of time writing what looked like chicken scratches in his notebooks. I opened one when he was out and tried to read it. I think he wrote math equations, but I never knew for sure.

I told a girlfriend about him once, and she said that maybe he was in the witness protection program. That made sense to me because he always was looking over his shoulder as if he feared someone was following him. Shortly before you were born he simply disappeared."

"Can you tell me anything else about him? Anything would help me. I thought about him so often while growing up, but I never could fill in a face. Do you have a picture?"

"I destroyed his picture many years ago on a day when I was feeling sorry for myself. As I said, he looked just like you –same blond hair and blue eyes and muscles. He had this cute way of crinkling up his eyes when he looked at me. He said he saw me in pink."

"He said that? He said he saw you in pink?"

Vivian nodded. "Yeah. Once he said he saw someone in black and it seemed to scare him. He spoke very good English like he was educated, but he had a slight accent. I never could figure it out, and he never admitted to being from anywhere else."

The two talked for another hour, but Jack learned little more about his father. Vivian's life had been a series of one bad decision after another. She never had given up, though, and she had always worked because she hated the idea of welfare. Jack gave her his phone number, and they promised to stay in contact. While Vivian soothed one ache that Jack lived with since he was small, he still wondered about his father. Why would he leave so suddenly? Why would he not follow up with at least one letter? Where did he go? Was he married? There were more questions than answers, especially since John probably wasn't his real name.

Chapter 10

Jack had the feeling he was running around in circles and, in fact, he was. He found Interstate 8 completely jammed, and he drove through the stop and go traffic with his fingers drumming on his steering wheel in frustration until he could exit at College. He drove toward the new Physics and Astronomy building and into the crowded visitor parking lot. He had one major advantage over all the others looking for parking, though, and that was the disability placard in his glove department. He carefully placed it on his dashboard and pulled into a roomy handicapped parking spot. The placard was only good for one more month, so why not use it?

He climbed the stairs to the fourth floor and then headed down the hall toward his father's office. He knocked on the door and braced himself, vowing to try to keep his promise to his mother and not have another argument.

He heard sounds coming from inside, including a man's voice clearly raised in anger, but couldn't make out the words. His father's softer voice replied in what sounded like a conciliatory tone meant to calm the other person, but it only seemed to infuriate the man still further. Jack caught those last angry words as the door opened.

"You're going to be damned sorry if you don't change your mind. This is your last chance!"

The door opened and a middle-aged man wearing an expensive looking suit brushed by Jack and strode down the hall toward the elevator. He looked vaguely familiar.

Professor Aaron Starling opened the door and stared up at his son, his eyes magnified by the dark-framed glasses that balanced precariously on his substantial nose. Short, balding, and about twenty pounds overweight, he stepped aside and Jack eased by him. Befitting a full professor who directed several graduate students, his corner office offered a view of the campus and mountains behind it. Professor Starling sat behind his desk and motioned for his son to take the chair facing it.

"I'm sorry you had to witness that. If I'd known what he really wanted, I wouldn't have accepted the endowed chair."

Then Jack realized whom he'd seen. "That's John Anderson?"

The professor nodded sadly. "He's crazy. Let's not go into that right now. To what do I owe this very rare pleasure?"

"Mom told you that she found one of my biological parents?"

"She did." Jack waited, but his father didn't continue. The silence grew. "You know I love you and Mom. This is just something I needed to do. If nothing else, I'd like to know what kind of health history runs in my family."

"You mean your real family?"

"No, you and Mom will always be my real family. I've told you that more times than I can count. I just don't know how to get through to you."

"We don't see much of you. Even though you're all grown up, we still worry about you."

"I understand that. Look, did Grandpa tell you to become an astrophysicist?

"No, you know that he wanted me to go into the family business."

"He didn't see any use for all that schooling, did he?"

Professor Starling smiled. "It was difficult for him to understand why anyone would want or need that much education since he only made it through the eighth grade."

"I just wanted to see whether or not I could cut it as a SEAL. Did you know that there's a 98% dropout rate?"

"I didn't know that, but you're capable of being successful at anything you try. As I remember, you did very well here."

"I just needed to get away."

"Suzie still drops by occasionally and asks about you."

"Let's keep her out of this. I'm here. No phantom father will ever take your place. Am I getting through to you?"

Professor Starling studied his son and then his own face began to crumble. He rose as tears cascaded down his face, and he hugged his son. Jack held him tightly, and he could feel his father's body shake through his sobs. He gained control slowly until finally he broke away from his son and dabbed his cheeks with a handkerchief.

Jack looked at his father's whiteboard and saw it covered with mathematical symbols. He studied them and recognized some of the differential equations.

"It looks like you're back to your theory of quantum teleportation. I recognize the Bob and Alice equations."

Professor Starling smiled with pride. "I don't know how many people who haven't taken graduate level physics classes would recognize that. You're right. I've had a breakthrough of sorts regarding entanglement. I'm scheduled to present my new paper this next month in New York. What are you up to?"

Jack bit his lip. He didn't want to ruin what up to now had been unusually pleasant. "Remember how we used to go to planetarium nights at the Reuben Fleet? They had a great show the other night about the possibilities of finding life on other planets, your favorite subject."

Professor Starling's eyes brightened. "Well, if my theory holds, someday we'll be able to visit some of those places without spending lifetimes getting there."

"I thought about that. Are you up on the latest candidates for alien life?"

Professor Starling nodded. "Sure, probably more up-to-date than NASA would like me to be. I think I've taken you to every science fiction movie where there's at least one alien; unfortunately, most don't do a good job making aliens credible. We've had that conversation before."

"I know. Anyway, I think the movie listed a couple of planets named Kepler-62e and some planet named Gliese with a number after it."

Starling reached for his pen and notepad and doodled as he talked. "The Kepler designation means that the planets have been located via the Kepler telescope. The Gliese 677 planet is a bit more interesting, though. Did the film explain where it's located?"

"No, at least I don't remember." Jack felt pleased that he'd managed to turn his father's attention away from his current unemployed status.

Professor Starling rose and walked to a star chart on the wall next to the whiteboard. He pointed at a star group over the Southern hemisphere.

"It's in the Scorpio constellation. The Sumerians described it 5000 years ago. They said it was at war with Osiris. Interesting, isn't it?"

"I don't understand."

"Well, the implication is that this star system was at war with another star system. It's kind of a very early version of *Star Wars*."

"Well, at least it's not the Death Star."

Professor Starling frowned. "No, I think our own particular Death Star is a lot closer."

"What do you mean?"

"I can't really talk with your mother about this...situation. It's a shame evangelicals let their religious fervor interfere with science. I'm not that eager for the Apocalypse to come. Let's just say that aliens are a lot closer than anyone thinks."

"You wouldn't say that to your undergrad class."

Professor Starling bit on his pipe stem and shook his head. "No, of course not. They'd take it, distort it, report it and then I would be put out to pasture. It's bad enough that people sensationalize what I write." He stared at his son before continuing. "Getting back to the Sumerians, you're bright enough to understand the truth that could lie beneath the myth."

"You think the Sumerians were aware of alien races in those two star systems?"

Professor Starling studied the star map and then leaned over to get a better view before continuing. "It's just far too much of a coincidence after all these years that using the latest science we have now, we've identified those same two star systems as having planets in the 'Goldilocks zone.'"

Jack thought for a minute as he remembered something. "Did the Sumerians ever describe the people from Scorpio, the ones from Gliese 677?"

Professor Starling smiled, rose, and walked over to his bookshelf. He ran his fingers over several books before pulling a massive volume that looked very scholarly and very dusty. He blew the dust off and returned to his desk where he began flipping through the book until he finally stopped at a specific section. He turned the heavy book on his desk at an angle so Jack could see the pages.

"Look for yourself. This was painted on a stone wall over 5000 years ago and depicts one of the 'Gods' they worshipped."

Jack studied the picture while his father continued while unconsciously adopting the tone of voice he used when he lectured.

"It's pretty clear that the artist drew a fair-haired God surrounded by dark Sumerians. Notice how bulked up he is compared to those around him. He looks a lot like you, doesn't he?" Professor Starling said as he turned his attention back to his pipe while Jack stared at the picture.

"Maybe, but it also could be a fair-haired Greek paying the Sumerians a visit."

"True. I know you think you've done a great job of distracting me from the subject very dear to my heart, but indulge me for a minute. Is there any chance you might return to school? I understand the job market is tough right now."

"I don't see an avalanche of offers for grad students with Masters' degrees in math or physics. I'd have to get a Master's degree followed by a PhD, and then my choices would be teaching and conducting research or doing government work behind a desk. I'm not sure I'm a good fit for either."

Professor Starling took the pipe from his mouth and his lips and rotated it in his hand before continuing. "It's nice we can have a conversation like the old days. I understand, believe it or not, that you don't want to follow in my footsteps."

Jack started to deny it, but his father raised his hands and continued.

"It's okay. I've helped raise you, so I know you're far more a man of action than I ever was. You played football, and that's something I never could do. You became a SEAL, and I would have washed out the first day. I can't see you as a professor, and I can't see you sitting all day at a desk. Does that surprise you?"

Jack nodded, stunned. "Yeah, it does. Why have you been pushing me to go to grad school, then?"

"Well, we never got this far, so I couldn't explain. We'll hear in a few months about a special program Larry Simon and Bill Weber proposed to NASA. The idea is to take the brightest graduates in math and physics and offer a specialized advanced degree to train astronauts.

The graduates would intern with NASA. They'll need a lot of newly minted astronauts to

96

train for the upcoming space shuttle as well as the trip to Mars a few years later."

"You never said anything about it."

"I never got this far. Just think about it. We'll know by September if we get the grant. I don't have to remind you that Larry and Bill are two of your biggest fans. Since my name is not on the grant application, there's no hint of nepotism although maybe they might think by taking my son they'll be able to muzzle me some. I did write the application entrance requirements, though, and you're a perfect match." Professor Starling smiled like a cat that had just swallowed the family's canary.

"Mom knows about this?"

"She doesn't know the details. She just thinks I want you back in school in some kind of conventional program. You'd hate it. This, though, requires someone who is way above average physically as well as mentally. Will you think about this?"

Jack nodded. His father looked at his watch. "I have an hour or so before my grad seminar. Why don't you walk with me to the food court and we'll grab something like old times."

"Sure, I must have been thirteen the first time you took me there."

Professor Starling put an arm around his son's massive shoulders and led him out the door. "The food isn't any better now, but it's still fast and cheap enough."

As the elevator descended, they both heard what sounded like firecrackers going off.

"I wonder what the celebration is?" Professor Starling said.

97

Jack's arm tightened around his father. "I doubt there's any cell reception here in the elevator. When we reach ground level, call 911. Tell them where you are. Those are gunshots."

"What are you going to do?"

"Don't worry about me. I have a graduate degree in handling myself in situations like this. I'll be fine. I'm going to see if someone needs help. Stay by the elevator and keep the door open while you talk to 911. Be ready to close the door and go up if anyone approaches with a gun."

"I don't want you to put yourself in any danger."

"I'll be fine."

When the door opened, Jack looked down the hall. He didn't hear any more shots, so he walked as quietly as he could while stopping at each door and listening. He reached Lecture Hall 1 and heard a loud voice, but he couldn't make out the words. Rather than open the door, he crept around the corner until he found the side door he remembered from when he took Abnormal Psychology. The door opened to a small room in the back of the platform where lecturers stood.

Jack entered the small storage room and then opened the door to the stage a crack and heard the voice more clearly now. He squinted and saw a tall thin man with wispy blond hair who looked to be in his late twenties. He stood with one hand clutching a rifle. Sitting in a chair beside him was Professor Bill Weber. His normally immaculately brushed hair stood in all directions while his glasses hung low on his nose. Jack could see the room was packed with students.

"I should be teaching you, but apparently I'm not deemed good enough. This man here is one of three people who failed me on my PhD qualifying exam. He's ruined my life, and now I'm going to publicly execute him for crimes against humanity. You all are here to serve as witnesses. I'll shoot anyone who moves or tries to help him. Put your cell phones and your computers down. If I see anyone trying to call or text, I'll kill you as well. Put your hands in your laps and just listen while I describe the tyranny of a select few who want to keep talented people like me from becoming teachers."

Jack studied the man and realized he was a trip wire ready to explode. He held the rifle so tightly that his knuckles were turning white. Soon he'd shoot Professor Weber and probably take out a few students before killing himself.

Jack's SEAL training had drilled into him that anything properly used could serve as a weapon. He looked around him until his eyes fell on a lone bridge chair stacked against a wall. It wasn't much, but it was metal; maybe it could stop a bullet. Jack picked it up and hefted it before deciding it would have to do. He looked out at the audience through the barely open door and prayed no one would call attention to him.

He decided that he'd have to move without any hesitation and trust his instincts. He'd risk everything on an attack from the side and hope that an amateur would not react in time. The man stood about ten feet away and would see him out of the corner of his eye. *How fast could the man turn and*

99

fire? Jack took a couple of slow calming breaths and felt his muscles ready themselves.

Jack burst through the door and rushed toward the man. He flung the chair so that it flew in a direct path toward the man's face as he turned in the direction of this unexpected attack. A shot rang out, but Jack already was on top of the man. He tackled him and wrestled the rifle away.

Jack held the man down while motioning for two men in the front row to join him on stage. He then had them sit on the man. He carefully unloaded the rifle and placed it on the lectern. Just then the main door to the auditorium burst open and several heavily armed men rushed in. The SWAT team was dressed for an assault.

It took an hour before the police were finished interviewing Jack. He then joined his father who stood a few feet away smiling broadly. "Let's get something to eat now. I'm sorry I didn't get to see you in action."

"There wasn't very much to see. This guy probably will get committed to a loony bin and never serve any time."

Professor Weber, his shoulders still shaking, joined them. "I don't know how to thank you, Jack. I really believe Gunter would have pulled the trigger."

"I'm glad I was here. I never realized being a professor could be such a dangerous occupation."

"I never thought it was. Did your father tell you about my grant proposal?"

"He did."

"Good. You were at the top of my list before this happened, just so you know. I can't thank you enough. When Mary finds out what you did, she'll want to thank you as well."

"It's fine. You don't owe me anything."

He and his father walked to the food court. They ordered their favorites and sat together. It felt like old times to Jack; he hadn't realized how much he missed his old man.

Professor Starling ate silently for a few minutes while he seemed to be debating something. Finally he sighed and pulled a notepad from his jacket pocket and wrote something down. He tore the page from the pad and handed it to his son.

"Maybe it's a good thing I have a SEAL in my family although I think John Anderson is all bluster. I don't take any of his threats seriously."

"Threats?"

"He wants me to take part in a lunatic project." Jack noted that his father seemed to be smiling at his own choice of words.

"That sounds dangerous."

"As I said, I don't take him seriously, but just in case, I want you to keep Gerald's name and phone number safe. If anything happens to me, talk with Gerald. He will fill you in. I don't want to go over it now because it's really nothing for you to worry about."

"Can't you just tell Anderson to take back the endowed chair and stuff it?"

"It's not that easy. Dean Williams is fond of the extra money, and some of the trustees aren't very happy that anyone who does a Google search on 'extraterrestrials' is likely to find something I've said or written. I think he would choose having someone else occupy the chair rather than give up the endowment. I don't want anything to interfere with the paper I plan to read at the conference. It's something I've worked all my life to achieve. I'd like to put this issue on the back burner until after the conference."

Jack glanced at the sheet of paper his father handed him before placing it in his wallet. It wasn't like him to be so dramatic.

"Who is this guy?"

"He's someone who keeps a very low profile. Don't call him unless you find it necessary."

"I've never known you to be so secretive."

"It's not something I enjoy. It's hard to know whom to trust nowadays. I've had colleagues try to avoid me lately. I suspect some government agents are questioning them about me."

"Why would the government care about your research?"

Professor Starling put a small hand on his son's muscular arm. "Things are very complicated. I can't go into now, but maybe we could meet for lunch off campus when I get back from the conference. I'll explain everything even though it will take some time. What's your security clearance?"

"Top secret."

"What I will tell you is far above that, but I plan to go to the press anyway."

"They'll lock you up and throw away the key."

"Not when this becomes public."

Jack looked at his watch and realized there was still time for one last errand. Luckily it wasn't more than a couple of freeway stops away. He hugged his father and told him to call him if his situation

102

became worse. They'd have that lunch date right after the conference.

Chapter 11

Jack drove to the Java Coffee Emporium in North Park. Located between a used car lot and a pawnshop with bars on its windows, the coffee house gave off a distinctly non-Starbucks vibe. Everything about the place emphasized that it was part of the local community, including a wall covered with pictures drawn with crayons by students at a local elementary school. The pictures hung on a wall adjacent to a small raised platform where local musicians performed. The sound of coffee being ground interrupted muted conversations.

The lack of a parking lot suggested that the locals walked to this place; outsiders had to find parking on the street. A teenaged girl with bright red hair and a nose ring directed Jack to a back room that also served as meeting place for community events. A small balding man with a thick black mustache sat at a table in the front of the room going through his slides on a laptop while many in the audience in the crowded room carried on whispered conversations.

Jack studied the audience as still more people streamed in. An anorexic-looking blond with her hair cut very short and a male teen with a bad case of acne, both clad in coffee house T-shirts, began bringing in additional folding chairs. A mild looking man with long blond hair tied in a neat ponytail walked to the front and welcomed everyone and introduced the presenter as Arnold Pearson, a man who had successfully hunted aliens for years and recently self-published a book about his adventures.

A staff member lowered the lights slightly so that the audience could see Pearson's slides reflected on the white screen on stage. Pearson spoke so haltingly that it was painful for Jack to listen. He described being abducted by aliens when he was much younger, and then he described his discovery that they had planted a tiny transmitter in his head.

Jack began to question why he had come. Of course it was possible that aliens did do something to Pearson to disrupt his thoughts, but it was just as likely that he suffered from a mental condition since he couldn't finish his own sentences. Pearson kept projecting new slides onto the screen while his voice droned on in a soft monotone. Jack looked around the room and his heart stopped. In the back row, he saw Cassandra sitting between two older women. *What was different about her?* Then it hit him. She no longer had a purple bruise covering half her face. She focused so completely on the speaker's words that she didn't seem aware of Jack staring at her.

He heard the word *Dulce* and turned his attention back to the speaker. The man claimed aliens took him there and tortured him. He gave no information on how he escaped. Jack studied the man and doubted he could have fought his way out of a room filled with marshmallows. He realized he was wasting his time and decided he'd wait in the coffee area until Cassandra came out. He turned and saw she had vanished.

105

Jack rose and hurried down the aisle toward the exit as several people craned their necks in his direction. He burst into the coffee serving area and looked for her, but she was gone. He moved quickly to the door and looked down both sides of the block. When he heard a car down the block start and drive in his direction, Jack walked to the sidewalk's edge and studied a dark model sedan as it approached him; he recognized Cassandra in the passenger seat next to one of the older women he had seen in the coffee house.

"Cassandra! Stop! We need to talk!" Jack shouted. As the car passed, the woman looked directly at him and stared without any show of emotion. *It's as if we never met,* he thought.

Jack took his keys from his pocket and ran to his car, gunned the engine, and drove in the direction Cassandra's car had taken. He hung back so she wouldn't realize he was following her. Once and for all he was going to find out more about her. The car carrying Cassandra continued on crowded North Park Boulevard before pulling onto Dairy Road. A succession of sad looking business parks and strip malls replaced the bright lights of the major thoroughfare. When he saw two bright headlights from a large vehicle coming up behind him much too rapidly for comfort, he pulled off the road into a quiet strip mall.

The lights belonged to a large dark-colored van that accelerated until it was right behind Cassandra's car. Jack watched as a side door opened on the van and a figure stuck something out and aimed it at Cassandra's car. Jack felt his heart beating too fast for comfort, and he began to feel sweat drip down his forehead. There was a bright flash of light and then Cassandra' car exploded into a fireball. The van roared passed the car and soon disappeared. Jack drove up to the car that now was fully engulfed in flames. He tried to approach it so he could help the two occupants, but the heat was too intense and he felt his face begin to burn.

Jack jumped back into his car and backed up to a safe distance just as he heard sirens in the distance. An explosion sent pieces of the car high in the air before they began to rain down. The former SEAL had seen enough destruction to know nobody could have lived through that firestorm. His hands shook as he did a U-turn and headed toward home knowing that Cassandra was gone. Whoever tried to kill her before now finally had succeeded. He didn't want to stick around and talk to the police.

Jack was so lost in his thoughts of Cassandra that he almost missed his freeway exit. The loss was so profound that he wondered whether a person's heart really could break from such a loss. No matter how much Paxil he took, it wouldn't help ease his pain.

Chapter 12

Jack drove back to his apartment on automatic pilot as images of Cassandra flashed through his mind. He realized as he pulled into the parking lot that he didn't even remember getting on or exiting the freeway. He dragged himself up the stairs to his apartment where he saw images of Cassandra everywhere he looked. Her presence still lingered in his bedroom. He had thought there would be plenty of time for them, but now someone had snatched that time away. He felt like screaming his rage but at the same time he longed to find the killers and unleash his fury on them. Realistically he knew he didn't have a single clue, no physical description of them and no memory of the van's license plate. Still, he couldn't give up so he tried repeatedly going over everything he could remember; there had to be something, some way to track down the people who murdered her. No matter what he did to them, though, it wouldn't bring back Cassandra who now was gone forever.

He found his bottle of Jack Daniels, poured himself a generous portion, downed it and started to reach for the bottle when his thoughts turned to Moon. There would be time to mourn Cassandra after he rescued his buddy. He had to compartmentalize all his grief and then open that compartment at a later time when he could give it his full attention. Now he had to think about poor Pete because rescuing him couldn't wait until a time in the distant future when he would be able to lift the sadness that threatened now to overwhelm him.

It had always been that way whenever he lost a member of his team during an operation.

He spent the rest of the evening developing a tactical plan for Dulce while he read over portions of Hawk's books and took notes. Even if he managed to collect everything on the list of equipment needed for the mission, the odds for success wouldn't be that good. He took a sleeping pill and slept that night with his gun tucked under his pillow.

Jack took Goldstone's printout the next morning and drove toward what he hoped was the location for the first team member on his list. Southeast San Diego is not a safe place, even in the daytime. As he drove deeper into the heart of the territory controlled by one of the toughest Mexican gangs in the entire country, he saw shabby streets filled with liquor store after liquor store along with small tract houses with postage stamp lawns now yellow from lack of care. All the houses seemed to have large dogs that growled and barked as he drove past them. Middle- aged women and kids waited at crowded bus stops while young men stood outside liquor stores and stared at him. Jack's car's navigation system finally announced he reached his destination just as he saw the shabby looking bar and grill on his right. Two young Hispanic men with enormous inked arms stood outside as silent sentinels. Jack knew they would search him, so he locked his gun along with the alien weapon in his glove compartment. The gang members eyed Jack as he climbed out of his car and locked it. They seemed amused that he thought a simple car alarm could keep them out of a car if they wanted something inside.

As Jack walked toward the door, the men drew closer together to block entrance to the building. He saw that both of them were armed and figured several more of the gang probably loitered inside. This wasn't the time or place for a one-man assault, so he stopped a few feet from the guards.

"I want to see Ricky. Tell him Jack Starling wants to see him."

"Maybe he doesn't want to see you," one of the men snarled.

Jack rolled up his sleeve so the men could see the triton tattoo on his arm. "We're brothers. We served in the same unit. He's going to be pissed if you don't tell him."

One man whispered something in the other's ear. They continued to whisper until the one closest to the door nodded and turned to go inside. The other man took a couple of steps toward Jack.

"You know the drill. Put your hands up and lean against the wall so I can pat you down. Nobody, not even Ricky's mother, gets to see him without me checking first."

The way in which the man searched him revealed the guard was a professional. *Nobody could have hidden a weapon that would not be detected with such a thorough search*, Jack thought with some admiration. Just as he lowered his arms, the door opened and a short, heavily inked Hispanic man built as solidly as a fire hydrant sauntered out. He looked amused.

"Amigo, come on in." The two guards stepped aside, and Jack entered the dimly lit bar. "Come into

110

my office," the man said and led Jack to a small back room that consisted of a desk and chair with two folding chairs facing the desk. He sat and motioned for Jack to take one of the folding chairs. AK 47s and boxes of ammo lay stacked next to the wall behind the desk.

Ricky Garcia folded his massive arms and stared at Jack. "Man, we sold out for you, and then you just disappeared."

"My shrink told me she'd cut off all my meds if I talked with you guys. She said it was the only way I'd ever get over my nightmares."

"So, just like that you ditched us? One day we're brothers and the next day we're garbage?"

"I'm sorry. Things got real bad, and I thought if they got any worse they'd lock me up in the loony bin and throw away the key."

"So, why did you come here now? I bet you need something, right?"

Jack nodded. "Yeah, Moon saw some things he shouldn't have seen while he was doing some contract work. A bunch of goons, including our buddy Scarpo, grabbed him and locked him up at a super-secret base. If we don't get him out soon, they'll kill him."

"So? I'm supposed to drop everything? You're not my team leader anymore. I've got my own team now." Ricky waved his arms in the direction of the door leading to the bar.

"Moon saved both our asses and you know it. We can't leave a brother behind. I'm going to do this with you or without you. The odds I succeed are much higher with you."

A smile slowly painted itself across Ricky's face. "Damned right your odds go up. I've got more firepower here than half our old unit."

"I'm surprised the Navy didn't get suspicious when you knew more about demolition than the guys instructing us."

"Tell me more about Moon."

Ricky settled back in his chair while his eyes bore into him. Jack knew that those eyes had witnessed countless deaths and executions without emotion. Ricky killed men with as little emotion as exterminators stamped out bugs. He knew more about high explosives than anyone Jack had ever met.

Ricky had been the second in command to a gang chief who had a reputation as a homicidal maniac. When war broke out and rivals assassinated his boss, Ricky became a marked man. He joined the Navy with a price on his head. His gang gained new members and avenged the death of its leader during the time he served with Jack. When he came back to San Diego, he realized there was a power vacuum, and so he took over. His SEAL training made him even more lethal than when he had left the gang.

Jack described his meeting with Moon, Scarpo's comments, and then what he'd learned about Dulce. Ricky's eyes didn't waver and he didn't interrupt, although Jack thought he saw the eyes narrow slightly when he described the aliens and the experiments on people. Finally he finished with what Maurice told him.

"So what's the plan and who's going to be part of this?"

"I want you, and I'm going to talk with Bill and Paul."

"You know how I feel about Bill."

"I know, but we'll never find anyone better at what he does. All that other stuff doesn't matter now."

"It does to me. That slot should have been mine, and you know it!"

Jack sighed. "I agree, but Tony made the decision. You saw my recommendation. I pushed for you."

Ricky's face softened a bit. "I know you did, and we're still tight. If Bill says anything at all to me, you're going to have to get by with one less team member. As far as Paul goes, I doubt the ball and chain will let him out of the house."

"You mean Mary?"

"Yeah, I'm sure his old lady still pussy-whips him. I doubt she lets him take a whiz without permission."

Jack took out a notepad from his pocket and scribbled something on a sheet before ripping it out and handing it to Ricky. "Here's my address and a date and time. Whoever is going will meet up then and we'll go over the plan."

Ricky rose and bumped fists with Jack. "I'm in because Moon's one of us; the rest is just frosting on the cake. I'd love a chance to blow away Scarpo without having to worry about a court martial."

Jack walked past the two guards who now eyed him with curiosity and headed to his next stop. He'd have to handle Larson with kid gloves. He drove to a business park near San Diego State where a sign for LANEX pointed to the back of the complex.

113

Jack parked and pushed through the glass doors where he saw a young receptionist with long blond hair and heavy blue eye shadow. She wore a light blue LANEX polo shirt and greeted him with a smile.

"Could you page Bill Larson for me?"

"Do you have an appointment, sir?"

"No, but tell him Jack Starling would like to see him." The pretty blond picked up the receiver and dialed an extension.

She whispered into it and then looked up and smiled. "He'll be right down."

Jack felt out of practice, but he sensed she was flirting with him. A few minutes later, a well-built man of medium height walked toward them. His short-cropped brown hair suggested a military history while his broad shoulders and probing eyes confirmed it. Larson's features were too broad for him to be considered handsome. His nose was a bit too wide and his mouth turned down in a perpetual frown. The two men embraced. Larson picked up a guest pass from the receptionist and handed it to Jack to wear. He then led him to an elevator. They waited until they were inside the elevator before speaking.

"What do you do here?"

"I'm head of security. It sounds a lot more important than it really is. Most of the guys working for me are too out of shape to chase down anyone. It's pretty routine."

"Hey, it's a job. I'm still looking."

"I haven't seen you since we were released," Larson said and made it sound like an accusation rather than a statement of fact.

114

Jack sighed and described his shrink's threat to cut off his meds if he opened up his wounds by having contact with his team.

"Nightmares? Yeah, I still get them too."

"Are you getting some help?"

"No. I'll get through it. Why come see me now? Aren't you afraid you'll lose your pills if you talk to the big bad sniper?"

"Pete Moon is in big trouble. I'm putting together the team to save him."

"Is the spick on your list?"

"Bill, come on. That part of our lives is over. You won. You got the promotion."

"It wasn't discrimination. I deserved it."

"Ricky's cool about working with you because he wants to save Moon. Pete's saved Ricky's ass just like he's saved all of us including you."

The elevator stopped and Larson led Jack to a set of doors marked SECURITY. The interior housed several small offices. He walked to one marked DIRECTOR and motioned for Jack to sit down in one of two chairs placed around a small table. Larson took the other chair.

"So what's happened to Moon?" Jack went into the details including the aliens at Dulce. "No shit? So, a stomach shot really put the dorks out of commission."

"The Draconians, not the dorks."

"Whatever. You always were the man with the plan. What's the plan?"

Jack picked up one of Larson's business cards on the table and wrote his address, a date and time on the back and handed it to him. "Will you be able to get some time off?"

"They owe me some vacation time so it won't be a problem. You were serious about all that alien stuff?"

"Yeah, I know it's hard to believe."

"This is so fucking great! I've been bored shitless here." Larson led Jack back to the receptionist desk and carefully removed his guest pass. "We can't allow anyone to walk out with these," he said.

Jack realized that Larson was putting on a show for the receptionist's benefit. She didn't seem to notice the wink he gave Jack.

The freeway traffic heading toward the seaside city of Del Mar was crowded as usual. Jack breathed a sigh of relief when he finally reached the Del Mar Heights exit. He turned right and headed to a large glass and metal building a couple of blocks from the big Del Mar Heights shopping center. He parked and found San Diego Discount Insurance Brokers listed in the large directory in the lobby. The elevator seemed to take forever so he finally decided to take the stairs up to the fifth floor.

The office contained dozens of tiny cubicles, each with a desk, a single chair, and just enough room for a phone and a laptop. Harsh fluorescent lights illuminated the work area. Men in white shirts and ties hunched over their computers while the women wore dark business suits. The place sounded like a beehive because of the hum of dozens of voices. A decidedly overweight blond female receptionist sitting behind the counter eyed Jack as if he were some kind of wildlife that had stumbled into the facility by mistake.

"Could I help you?"

"I'm looking for Paul Milburn. Please tell him Jack Starling is here."

The receptionist looked down at a directory and then gave Jack a perfunctory smile. "You can tell him yourself. He's on the third row from the left, the fifth cubicle down."

Jack followed her directions and saw Milburn, clad in a white shirt that seemed too tight for his large chest and shoulders and a red tie. His muscular thighs seemed to bulge out of his dark slacks. He looked up from his laptop display and stared blankly for a moment until he recognized his visitor and placed him as someone outside the context of his workspace.

"Jack? What the hell brings you here? I haven't seen you since the trial. I thought maybe you were back in the hospital or something."

"Yeah, it's been too long. Is this job Mary's idea?"

Milburn's face flushed. "Kind of. Her dad owns the agency. It's good steady pay."

Jack heard the defensiveness in his friend's voice.

"I'm glad. You're way better off than me because I'm still looking. Could you step out of the office for a few minutes? I need to talk to you about something confidential."

Milburn rose and looked over the cubicles before turning back to Jack. "I'm entitled to a coffee break. You go downstairs and I'll meet you in a few minutes. There are some tables and chairs around the side next to the little deli that's closed right now."

Jack found a table under an umbrella and waited a few minutes before he saw Milburn coming down the stairs. He still moved like a leopard. It struck him that seeing his friend in that insurance agency full of tiny cubicles reminded him of some noble predator locked in a tiny cage at a zoo while the life slowly drained out of him. He'd never understand women. Did Mary have to pussy-whip him to the point that he became nothing more than a domesticated cat or dog with none of the fierce warrior left inside him?

Jack studied his friend. Milburn's eyes had the same wariness they had when he and Jack were stalking through hostile villages, yet now he seemed concerned about some pencil pusher in the office catching him on a coffee break. Although he looked like a typical blond California surfer, his real talents lay in his ability to drive, fly, or fix anything mechanical. On top of that, he was a marksman and second only to Larson in the entire platoon when it came to shooting ability.

"Moon's in big trouble. A few of us are going in after him, but I know that could be a problem for you."

"What kind of trouble?"

Jack explained. Each time he repeated the story it sounded more unbelievable.

"You're serious?"

"Yes, I'm serious. Ricky and Larson are in. I think I know what Mary would say."

"Let me handle Mary. I took a vow with you guys. I'm about ready to go postal and start shooting up the office. I put in eight fucking hours a day pushing life insurance policies to people who

118

don't need them, and then I have to put up with Mary telling me that Daddy says I need to work harder so he can promote me."

Jack wrote out his contact information and the time and date of the meeting. They shook hands. As Jack drove home, he wondered whether Mary would figure out a way to stop Paul.

Chapter 13

Jack remembered the times Cassandra knocked softly on his door and part of him still waited for her do it once again while he went through the motions of putting together an operation. He'd developed tactical plans for his unit many times, but this time was different for two reasons. He couldn't get Cassandra out of his mind, and the enemy held one of his own team captive.

Why didn't Cassandra acknowledge him? If she did, maybe she'd be alive now. He remembered the last time they made love he'd promised himself that the next time she came over he'd pretend to doze off and then he'd follow her back to her place. He had wanted to know more about her. He hungered for her physically, but he also wanted to be more a part of her life even though he figured she was crazy. Now it was too late. He forced his mind back on the job at hand and spent four hours working on his tactical plan for Dulce. He studied the Dulce map in one of Hawk's books and realized that it wouldn't be a problem getting there; the special ID cards presented a challenge, though, and he couldn't figure out a way they could get around them. Shooting their way in would be a nightmare. He looked at his watch and saw it was eleven, and he remembered Cassandra's previous visits around that time. *Well, that wasn't going to happen anymore.*

Jack left his plans on the kitchen table and turned to head to his bedroom when he heard a soft knock. He looked through his peephole and froze. His mind had to be playing tricks on him. It couldn't be! He opened the door slightly and stared at a dead ringer for Cassandra or maybe it was her ghost. His mouth opened, but nothing came out. The woman squeezed past him and stood in living room with a quizzical look on her face. Jack's heart was beating so fast that he thought he'd have a heart attack. He shut and double locked the door and turned toward his guest.

What he saw made him freeze. A fading purple bruise still covered one cheek. The silence grew uncomfortable. Cassandra looked genuinely puzzled at his reaction.

"Is something wrong? Do I look strange?"

"It's your bruise. I saw you last night at a meeting and you didn't have the bruise. After that..." Jack found he couldn't describe what he'd seen, at least not to her or whoever she really was.

"What meeting? I didn't go to any meeting."

"At a coffeehouse. It was a meeting for a group called Aliens Among Us. I saw you sitting in the back row. I even yelled at you as you drove by after the meeting but you ignored me."

"I was home all night. You say you saw someone who looked like me?"

"Not someone who looked like you. She could be your identical twin except she didn't have a bruise on her face. Do you have a twin sister?"

Cassandra hesitated. "Not that I know of. Are you sure she looked like me?"

Jack threw his hands up in exasperation. "Don't play games with me. I'm beginning to think I'm going crazy. Can't you just level with me? Do you have a twin sister?"

Cassandra looked directly into his eyes with the same guileless expression he'd seen before. "I don't have a twin sister."

Cassandra wore a red sweater and jeans. *God, she looks good*, Jack thought. He smiled to try to hide his exasperation. He read once that everyone has a twin somewhere else on the planet; they just don't know it. Despite the astronomical odds against meeting that twin, he'd run into a dead ringer for her and watched as someone executed her. He felt so grateful that somehow she was here that he didn't want an argument to ruin their evening.

Cassandra continued as if nothing unusual had happened. "You told me that you see auras. Is that right?"

Maybe she thinks I'm crazy, Jack thought. "Yeah, but we don't need to talk about that. I'm sure that since you're a scientist, you'll just laugh at me. Most people don't believe me."

Cassandra looked troubled. "No, I believe you. All of us see in slightly different frequency bands; you just have inherited a broader range. It must run in your family. Did your father have that ability?"

"Apparently he did, but I don't really want to talk about him. He left before I was born, so he wasn't much of a man. He claimed he was a scientist, but now we'll never know."

"Did your mother describe him?" "She said he looked exactly like me. I'm a chip off the old block."

"And he just disappeared one day without any explanation?"

"Yeah. I just hope I'm a better person."

Cassandra eyebrows rose. "I'm sure you are. I'm here because I missed you. I want to spend the night. Is that okay with you?"

"Sure. I've missed you and hoped you'd come back. I really want us to be able to spend more time together." They moved closer to each other and then embraced. Jack easily lifted her and carried her to his bedroom. They were far more comfortable with each other's bodies by now. Jack decided he wanted to please her and focus on her pleasure, but Cassandra apparently had made a similar decision to focus on him. They spent an hour in slow lovemaking as they explored and touched each other tenderly.

Gradually the lovemaking grew more and more intense and noisy as Cassandra came multiple times. Finally she collapsed in Jack's arms. They both gasped for breath as they lay together for what seemed like an hour. Jack trained himself in Afghanistan to keep awake when he needed to do so because often his life depended on it.

Despite his body's eagerness to drift into a very pleasant unconsciousness, he forced himself now to stay awake by focusing on thoughts that would keep him from drifting off. Finally, with his eyes barely open, he caught a glimpse of his bedside clock and saw it was four in the morning. He felt Cassandra stir and he forced himself to lie motionless while he focused on breathing slowly and deeply to simulate sleep. When he felt her leave the bed, he pretended to roll in his sleep so he could watch her with his eyes opened just a crack. She dressed quickly and efficiently and then tiptoed out of the bedroom. Jack rolled out of bed and moved cat-like while putting on his clothes. He walked to the door and looked down the hall where he saw Cassandra standing at the kitchen table with her head bent down as she read his tactical plans for Dulce.

After several minutes of studying the plans, she took out her cell phone and dialed a number and then whispered something into the phone before hanging up. She spent another ten minutes studying the materials before leaving the apartment and closing the door softly behind her. Jack waited a couple of minutes and then quietly stepped outside. He saw her waiting in the parking lot. He moved from car to car, keeping his body bent low until he was able to hide behind his car. He watched as a white colored Ford Taurus drove up. Cassandra climbed in and the car headed toward the parking lot exit.

Jack climbed into his car and waited until the Taurus turned right and headed toward Park Avenue. He gunned his engine and turned out of the parking lot and then hung back several car lengths. Finally the Taurus pulled into the parking lot of an older two-story apartment building. A small bald man climbed out of the car and joined Cassandra as they walked side by side to an apartment. The man unlocked the door and they both entered.

Jack stared at the apartment and memorized its number. *Why would Cassandra care about his plans for Dulce? Was she some kind of government spy? Was this guy her partner or her husband and lover? What was she up to?* He didn't know, but he was going to find out. He drove home and double locked the door before climbing back into bed. He'd get some sleep because he would need it when he confronted Cassandra and her boyfriend later that day.

125

Chapter 14

Jack slept until noon and then spent much of the day making a list of weapons and other equipment they would need. He studied maps of the Dulce area and downloaded a map of New Mexico that he used to refine his plan several times before finally printing out copies for his team. SEALS didn't eat finger foods, so Jack made a quick trip to the Vons down the block and returned with chips, chicken wings, salsa, and beer. He looked at his watch and realized he still had time to confront Cassandra. He hated the idea that she might be part of a government spying operation. One way or the other, he would force the truth from her. Besides, given what she now knew about Dulce, he wanted to make sure she didn't spread the word and alert anyone that he was planning the raid.

Jack headed toward Cassandra's apartment. As he neared the complex, he thought about the possibility that government goons might follow him there. He checked his rearview mirror and side mirrors but didn't notice anyone tailing him. He found a parking spot and lingered for several minutes while he checked his mirrors to look for vehicles with telltale government license plates. Satisfied everything looked normal, he looked for signs of life as he approached Cassandra's apartment. Only a few blaring TVs broke the later afternoon silence. He wondered if she might be at work, wherever that might be. Come to think of it, he didn't even know exactly what she did or the name of the country she came from. Her accent sounded a bit Russian or maybe Romanian like the girl he met once who worked in the VA hospital.

Jack gave the door three loud knocks. He heard movement within the apartment and saw the shades part slightly before the door opened revealing the slightly built man he'd seen with Cassandra earlier that morning. Bald with no visible eyebrows, he reminded Jack of a picture of Humpty Dumpty he had seen in a book as a child. Dressed in jeans and a plain blue long sleeved shirt, the man stared at Jack as if he had seen a ghost. The silence grew uncomfortable until Jack finally broke it.

"I'm Jack. I know Cassandra lives here. I need to talk with her."

"She's not here, but she will return soon. My name is ...Mark. Please come in."

He walked past the man into a sparsely furnished room that contained a kitchen in the far corner and a hall that probably led to a bathroom and bedroom. *Why the hell didn't Cassandra mention him? Are they sleeping together?* Jack asked himself. He sat down in a chair next to a large bookcase. The furniture looked like rental stuff. He realized that the Taurus he saw early that morning probably was rented as well. The place lacked any sense of permanence. Jack decided that it looked barely lived in and didn't even have any discernible cooking odors.

"Are you her husband?"

The man shook his head but did not smile. "We work together. Would you like a drink while you wait? Cassandra has told me much about you." The man spoke in a toneless almost robotic tone. Jack figured his English just wasn't as good as Cassandra's.

"Water would be fine." Jack turned his attention to the books in front of him with the hope that they might reveal more about Cassandra. *Did she like mysteries or science fiction? Were there any cookbooks to show what kind of cuisine she enjoyed?* He saw several shelves of genetics textbooks that looked pretty advanced. His attention turned to the bottom shelf, and he stared as his mind registered the titles: *The Absolute Beginner's Guide to Sex, Make Love Like a Pro*, and *Kama Sutra Positions Illustrated*. He smiled; Cassandra was a fast learner. He became increasingly aware of a loud whining sound coming from what appeared to be a coat closet on the wall across from where he sat.

Mark returned shortly and placed a plastic glass of water on the coffee table. "Please drink. We rarely have guests. Is there anything else you would like?"

"No. I didn't mean to interrupt your work. Maybe I should go and return later."

The sound of a key in the door drew both men's attentions as Cassandra entered dressed conservatively in jeans and a loosely fitting dark green sweater. Today her eyes looked green rather than blue as she stared at Jack.

"This probably wasn't a good idea, but I wanted to see you again," he said.

"No, you just surprised me." She looked at her colleague and they seemed to exchange some kind of message because the man turned and headed down the hall.

"Did I say something wrong?" Jack said.

"No, Mark has a lot of work to do. There's no reason to be concerned about him. We work together but we're not lovers. Is that what's bothering you?"

"Uh...yeah. Does he live here with you?"

"Yes, he does because we work together."

"I thought after last night you'd be happy to see me again. It's probably a bad time for you, but I have something we need to discuss."

"Okay, but there is little more to know about me. How did you find my apartment?"

Jack felt his face flush. "I followed you this morning. After all, I have no way of getting in touch with you. I don't even have your cell number."

"You never asked." *How could someone that hot in bed be so cold in the light of day?* For a split second Jack wondered if maybe Cassandra had a twin sister. How else could you explain her lack of feelings?

"I would like for us to be honest from now on, and that means not keeping any secrets from each other."

Cassandra's eyes met Jack's direct gaze, and she didn't look away. "Of course, we should be honest with each other."

"Maybe we should start by having you explain why you're so interested in my tactical plans for Dulce."

"What do you mean?"

"I mean I saw you going over my plans."

"I don't understand. How did you see me?"

"It doesn't matter. Just answer my questions. Are you a government spy?"

"No, I'm not working for your government."

Jack thought for a minute and realized that she had parsed her sentence a bit too finely, and his gut told him she was holding back. "Then what government do you work for? Why do you care about Dulce?"

"It's...very difficult to explain. I would never hurt you. In fact, I want to help you."

"Try explaining."

Cassandra sighed. "I work for a friendly government that ordered me to stop what is happening at Dulce."

"The Brits?"

"No. Does it matter? Why can't you just trust me? Don't you care enough for me to trust me?"

"I can't trust you when you've deceived me from the very beginning. I feel like I walked into a foreign movie about an hour late, and now I'm trying to play catch up. You have an accent, cute as it is, and I want you to tell me where you're from. We can't have trust if you don't level with me."

Cassandra shrugged and pulled up a chair and sat facing Jack. He folded his arms defensively. He didn't want her beauty to distract him. He wanted answers, but he could feel himself becoming aroused just looking at her. He tried to drive those thoughts out of his head and think with his brain.

"As you know from my accent, I'm not from around here. I know from your plans that you find the idea of aliens difficult to accept. I'm from someplace far away, a distant planet. I'm not from Draco if that's what you're thinking. You've seen me naked, so you know that I don't change shapes. I look exactly the way you see me. I'm from a planet that your scientists haven't discovered yet."

Jack let his breath out very slowly and stared at her. "It's like I have to drag every word out of you. What's the name of your planet?"

"Using the sounds you can make, your people would call it Androvia."

"Let's say you're really an alien from Androvia, what do you want from us? The Draconians apparently want certain heavy metals as well as humans for their experiments according to the books I've been reading. What do you want?"

"The Draconians want much more than just trade. They're planning to take over your world as they have done with other worlds. We're their oldest enemies and simply want to keep your world free of them."

Jack shook his head. "I've been around the block a few times, and I know that nobody is completely altruistic. You want something, and clearly you want it bad. I can tell you're still not leveling with me."

Cassandra shrugged in a very human way. "We can't match their numbers. Right now only our technology keeps us free. You *must* believe me. The Draconians have made it difficult for our people. We've fought them for far longer than you can imagine, and we're losing. We need worlds with intelligent life as our allies and cannot permit another such world to fall into their hands."

"So you're not a real scientist studying genetics? That's just a cover?"

"I said it was complicated. I am a scientist, and I do study genetics. Our people are very advanced in that science, but I also have other talents. I'm a warrior like one of your SEALS."

131

Jack laughed. "You? It's hard for me to think of you as a warrior. I suppose you're going to tell me that Mark also is a warrior."

"No, but I really am, and I can help you. I have weapons such as the one you took from the Draconian, weapons that can make your mission more successful. I also can help you solve your biggest problem."

Jack crossed his arms in a challenging way. "What's that?"

"The ID cards. I told you that we have very good technology, good enough to create cards that will pass Draconian security."

"That's hard to believe. Why should I trust you that the cards will work?"

"Because I'm going with you, and my life will be in as much danger as yours. Actually the Draconians hate my kind even more than they dislike humans."

Jack's head was spinning. "Your name really isn't Cassandra, is it?"

Cassandra smiled, but it was a decidedly sad smile. "Now you're suddenly upset because Cassandra isn't my name? I chose that name because it pleased me. My real name would be meaningless to you."

"Try me."

Cassandra shrugged once again and then spoke in a tone far different than she had ever used before with him. Jack couldn't break the sound into syllables. What disturbed him was how such an alien sound came from someone who looked like her. His face mirrored his unease.

"So all the time we spent together was just your way of leading up to asking me to break into Dulce? All of our lovemaking was an act?"

Cassandra flushed. "I'm not very good with emotions, but I ... enjoyed the lovemaking. I really do care for you even though I have trouble expressing it. Love is something I still don't completely understand although I've read your books and seen your movies. Let's just say the rules for mating are very different where I come from. My original plan was to break into Dulce with Mark. We would have little chance of success, but I have my mission just as you had yours as a SEAL. You saved me from the Draconians, and I saw what a good man you are. I trust you with my life. If you tell anyone about me, your government will lock me up. They might even dissect me."

Jack stared at Cassandra while a fight raged in his head. One part of him felt hurt and used. It cried out to him, *hurt her as much as you can and then leave her. She's done nothing but lie to me since we've met. She probably considers me as no more a concern than a dog to train to do her bidding.* The other part still cared about her and wanted to believe she really did care for him. He had no reason to believe she couldn't help them succeed. He owed it to the Moon Man to rescue him. He mulled his options and reluctantly made his decision.

"Come over tonight around seven. That's when we're having our planning meeting. Leave out all the Androvian stuff. Let's just say that you're an ex-Mossad agent. It goes with your accent."

"Israel, right?"

Jack smiled and eyed her critically. "Yeah, I can't say you look Israeli, but tell them if they ask that your parents came from Sweden. You certainly could pass for Swedish."

Cassandra nodded and then smiled with a glint in her eye. "Do you like the way the Swedish women look?"

"I do. The girls there are a lot taller, but you would fit right in."

Cassandra walked up to Jack, lifted her head and kissed him softly on his lips before she turned with a mischievous smile on her face and headed to the door. Jack's eyes followed as he marveled at her grace. *Whatever else she is, she's definitely female,* he thought. She opened the door and stepped aside so he could leave.

As Jack walked down the stairs he thought, *I'm not sure what Cassandra really is, but she's sure as hell sexy.*

Chapter 15

Cassandra, now shorn of any makeup or lipstick, arrived first. She had dressed casually in loose jeans, worn tennis shoes, and a baggy gray sweatshirt. Jack looked at her approvingly. *She's smart enough to know that she needs to look ready for action and not too feminine*, he thought. Ricky came next. He also came ready for action sporting a bright red long-sleeve shirt that Jack identified as his friend's gang color. He mockingly did a double take when he saw Cassandra before leering at her.

"I didn't think you wanted us to bring dates."

"Cassandra used to work for the Mossad. She can take care of herself."

"I doubt it."

Cassandra moved with lightning speed. Her hands moved so quickly that they were a blur. Suddenly Ricky sank to his knees and struggled for air. Cassandra had one finger on his throat. She removed the finger casually and stepped back. Color slowly came back to Ricky's face. He rose to his feet and glared at her.

"Sorry, I just wanted to show you that I can take care of myself," she said softly.

Ricky's dark eyes bore into her but a smile slowly spread over his face. She had taken a few steps back to show she meant him no harm. He spoke in measured tones that ensured no misinterpretation. "I think you'll do fine. Just remember the next time you try something like that, you better fucking be sure you finish the job because otherwise I'll put a bullet right between your eyes."

Cassandra studied him and then nodded just as the doorbell interrupted them. Jack saw that Larson and Milburn had arrived at the same time. He welcomed them and prepared to intervene as Larson and Ricky eyed each other. As they moved toward each other, Jack stepped between them.

"Let's concentrate on saving Pete. We don't have to love each other, but we have to watch each other's back while we're on the mission. After that, you guys can settle your differences anyway you want."

"Then the sooner this is over, the better," Larson said.

"Yeah, it can't end soon enough for me. I don't even want to be in the same room with you any longer than it takes," Ricky said.

Jack noticed how Ricky dropped his hand to the pocket that bulged. Sure enough, violence was a real possibility. He picked up a stack of papers and began distributing his handout.

"Let's get started," he said with as business-like a tone as he could muster.

Jack spent the next hour going through the logistics, pausing only to answer questions. He then turned to the equipment list. "Put your initials next to anything you can bring to the party. Some of this stuff is pretty expensive, but we'll figure out a way to get it."

Ricky looked at the list. "The weapons are no problem. Hell, I've got rocket launchers, sniper rifles, and enough ammo to start our own war. You name it. I even have some M60s and a couple of Carl Gustavs."

136

Larson studied the list and then spoke while looking at Jack and ignoring Ricky. "I'd love to get me a Carl Gustav. I can handle the transportation, and I know where I can get some uniforms and some insignia to match what you showed us in the book."

Milburn had been studying the list as well as the plan. "I can fly anything we steal there, and I'll put some holes in any aliens we find."

The group turned to Cassandra. She spoke in a very business- like way. "I can provide everyone with ID cards that will pass through Draconian security. I'll need each of you to give me your name and accurate weight. I also will provide some special equipment if we decide to go through an unmarked entrance."

"How do you know where those entrances are?" Milburn said.

"My team has been researching the aliens for quite a while, and I have GPS coordinates."

"Ask her to show you some fighting moves," Ricky said with a smirk.

"No, if Jack vouches for her, I'm fine," Milburn replied.

"I think I'm being watched, so you might want to shake off any tails when you leave," Jack said.

"You could have said something about that earlier," Larson said.

Just then the sound of squealing tires followed by the sound of heavy footsteps up the stairs caused everyone to turn toward the door. The men looked at one another and then backed away from it.

137

"Concussion grenades?" Milburn whispered. Ricky pulled a pistol from his pocket and casually stroked it.

"Yeah, maybe smoke also. They're probably heavily armed," Jack said. He reached in his pocket and took out his gun. He felt the presence of the little alien weapon. He fished it out and showed it to Cassandra.

"Let me have that. I can adjust the frequencies and handle whatever comes through the door," she whispered to him.

Jack handed her the weapon. He closed his eyes and stuck a finger in one ear and waited. The men knew the drill very well and prepared as best they could. Ricky dove into the hall that led to the bedroom.

The door exploded, rocked by the force of the grenades. Men dressed in SWAT attire including thermal imaging goggles rushed in. They staggered as they entered and then began to fall to the ground. Jack staggered a bit, but he saw that his men also fell to their knees and began retching. It took a few minutes for them to get over their nausea. As the ex-SEALS began to feel better, they saw the men comprising the SWAT team lay motionless on the floor.

Jack bent over one of them and leaned over to see whether he could catch a heartbeat.

"They're alive, just unconscious. I didn't think you wanted them dead. If you do, it's not a problem," Cassandra said casually without any hint of emotion. The men stared at her.

"How the hell did you do that?" Milburn said.

"It's one of the weapons my group confiscated from the aliens."

"Maybe we should finish the job," Ricky said as he eyed the bodies.

"They won't remember what happened because the weapon disrupts their neural receptors; it shorts out their electrical signals."

Jack saw Ricky studying Cassandra and decided he needed to take control. "We better get out of here while we still can because I'm sure reinforcements will be on the way when they don't report back. Meet me tomorrow at McCray Mortuary at six with whatever you can bring. I have a friend there who will help. We'll have to speed up our timetable. I'm not going to be able to come back here."

The others left. Cassandra remained as Jack grabbed a duffle bag from his closet and began stuffing it.

"You're pretty handy with that weapon," Jack said without looking up.

"I've had a lot of practice with it. I told you that I'm also a warrior."

"You didn't seem to be affected by the weapon. How different are you from us?"

"Not that different. All life forms broadcast at slightly different frequencies. That's why you couldn't see my aura. I think I've already proved to you that I'm pretty human. I bleed and die just like you."

"What about that woman who looked just like you? Are there others of your kind here?"

Cassandra hesitated. "There...might be. I don't know."

"Do you all look alike?"

Cassandra looked down. "We don't have as much physical variance as humans. We don't all look alike, though."

"Let's get out of here. Jack closed the duffle bag. When they reached his car, he hesitated and then bent down and looked under it. He checked each wheel carefully and then whistled as he felt something in a wheel well. He pulled out a GPS tracker and studied it before getting in the car. He drove to a nearby Ralph's supermarket and saw what he hoped to find. He stepped out of the car and placed the tracking device on the underside of a large delivery truck. He figured it soon would be heading toward central California to pick up more produce. That signal should keep the guys tracking him busy for a while. He drove toward Hawk's place.

Chapter 16

The mortuary looked deserted, so Jack drove around to the back of the small house and noted that no one could see his car from the street. He motioned for Cassandra to wait in the car. Hawk answered the door on the first knock wearing a black suit, white shirt, and red tie. He stepped aside and motioned for Jack to come in. He pointed to the kitchen table where an open book lay next to a plate holding a half-eaten sandwich. On the nearby kitchen counter a coffeemaker made happy sounds.

"Looks like you're dressed for business."

"We had two funerals back-to-back today. You want some coffee? You look like you need some."

Jack found a cup and filled it. The heat warmed his hands.

"Some government goons attacked me. I have a friend in the car that's going to be part of my team. Can we spend the night? The rest of my team will meet up here tomorrow night at six, and then we'll head to Dulce. I'm sorry to drag you into this, but I didn't know where else to turn. I'm sure they're staking out my parents' place.

"You're both welcome to stay here. I've got a couple of extra bedrooms and a sofa. Is there anything else I can do?"

"Let me bring in my friend and we'll talk. I really appreciate this. I feel funny imposing on you when we haven't seen each other in years."

"It's fine. It's a lot more exciting than putting a new coat of makeup on Mister Johnson."

Jack introduced Cassandra to Hawk. He noticed that Cassandra struggled to make small talk with his friend. He glanced at Hawk, who rolled his eyes.

Hawk tried again with Cassandra. "How do you know Jack?"

"We're lovers."

"Great," Hawk said and Jack winced when he saw his friend's face.

He tried to think of a way of distracting Hawk from his interrogation.

"You mentioned you were a scientist. What kind of scientist?"

"I study genetics."

"Do you work for a pharmaceutical company or the government?"

Cassandra paused before answering. "I work for my government."

"You speak very good English. What country are you from?"

"It's not important."

"I think it's very important. Would it make more sense for me to ask what planet you're from?" Hawk said.

Cassandra pressed her lips together but didn't respond.

Jack shrugged. "I should have just told you. Cassandra is from a planet called Androvia. They and the Draconians are enemies."

Hawk flushed with excitement. "This is so cool! I'm happy to help you any way I can."

"You've already done enough."

"I found some more books since the last time we talked. If their underground rail system runs on magnetic energy, it might be possible to disrupt it so they can't send reinforcements very quickly."

Cassandra gave Hawk her full attention. "What do you have in mind?"

Hawk picked up a pad of paper near his telephone and began sketching something. "However the Draconian trains work has to fit in with the physics of our planet, so that means we don't need anything alien to disrupt it. Here's what I'm thinking..."

Jack watched the two as they discussed how a magnetic disrupter could work and what it would take to build one. Hawk insisted he could pick up the parts needed in the morning from a Radio Shack. He spoke rapidly, almost hyperventilating from excitement.

"Do you mind if I make a couple of sandwiches?" Jack said once the conversation ebbed.

"Do you have any vegetables? I don't eat meat," Cassandra said.

"Is that true for all your people?" Hawk asked.

"We haven't eaten meat for a very long time. We're the only vertebrates left on our planet."

"Why don't you show us what you found while we eat?" Jack said.

Hawk left and returned a few minutes later carrying half-dozen books. "I guess it's a hobby of mine," he said apologetically. "I try not to mention it when I go on dates because it turns off women."

Cassandra looked at Hawk blankly.

Hawk saw Cassandra's face and added quickly, "I've found that women don't find me very attractive when I talk about the possibility of life on other planets."

"Either it's that or maybe it's the fact you spend all day with dead people," Jack said.

"It's a taboo to talk about death?" Cassandra asked.

Hawk brightened from her attention. "Yeah, we have all kinds of expressions to soften the impact. We say someone *passed away* or *went to his reward*, or even *went to meet his maker*."

Cassandra looked down at her fork that held a piece of lettuce and seemed to consider whether or not to reply before she finally spoke.

"That's silly."

"Not to anyone who loses a loved one," Jack said.

Cassandra shrugged. "They're not really *lost*. Death is just one of many states that coexist. Dying is little different from being born."

"It is to the person dying," Jack said.

Hawk stared at her and then slowly nodded. "Quantum physics! Of course you'd say that."

"You told me that you bled and died just like us," Jack said.

"I do. Death is too complicated for me to explain; I don't have the words. Maybe we should spend our time talking about your plan. I will need to stop by my apartment to pick up some equipment. We could do that tonight or on the way to Dulce."

"You have to let me come. I know I can help," Hawk said.

"Larson is bringing something large enough to hold us plus all the equipment. I guess we could squeeze you in. When the shooting starts, I don't want you to get in the way."

"I promise I won't. Don't forget that I used to go deer hunting with my dad. I'm not a SEAL, but I can hit a target."

"It's different when you shoot at a person and not a deer," Jack said.

"They're not human," Hawk said.

"He's right. They aren't human," Cassandra added emphatically.

"Okay, now what about the books you found? What can you tell us we don't already know?" Jack said. They talked far into the night with Cassandra correcting some of the errors in Hawk's books.

Chapter 17

Larson had known exactly what they needed. Drivers didn't bother to give the battered dark beige van he drove a second look. Ricky arrived shortly afterward and removed the cover to his truck bed, revealing an arsenal that drew Jack's whistle of appreciation. He moved to help unload the weapons.

"Mine will not take up much room," Cassandra said as she eyed the hardware much the way a used car salesman eyes a trade-in he intends to undervalue. She touched the Carl Gustav and looked at Jack.

"It's an 84 recoilless anti-personnel weapon. It will go through armor like a knife through butter."

Cassandra smiled. "Size is not always that important. I'm bringing something much smaller that's much more powerful."

"Don't ever say size doesn't matter. It matters plenty to the women I know," Ricky said with a suggestive smile.

Cassandra eyed him. "The women you know must be very easily satisfied. Haven't you ever heard that it's better to under promise and over deliver? My colleague is half your size and women pay him for his services."

Jack tried to hide his smile when a very deflated looking Ricky failed to respond. *She'd make a good standup comedian because she says everything so deadpan when she jokes. At least I hope she's joking*, he thought. He picked up one of the uniforms he saw bundled in the back of the van. "Just look at that insignia!" He pointed at a star and lightning bolt badge shoulder patch.

146

"It should match what your book showed the Army personnel wearing at the lower levels. I have a friend who's a genius when it comes to creating bogus badges," Larson said with a note of pride.

"It is the Draconian representation of their unity of worlds. The lightning shows what happens to any planet that attempts to declare its independence," Cassandra said.

The men stared at the badge. "Like the Death Star in *Star Wars*," Larson said.

"If they didn't need the heavy metal here, they'd use a weapon that powerful on this planet without a second thought," Cassandra said.

The men lapsed into silence. It took over an hour to load all the equipment as well as the men's duffle bags. Larson drove to Cassandra's apartment with Jack directing him. The men waited in the van for Cassandra until she reappeared. This time, Mark joined her as they dragged a large bag toward the parking lot where Ricky and Jack helped load it. Ricky stared at Mark and gave Cassandra a very skeptical look.

"He's an expert in alien biology," Cassandra said quickly and nodded to her colleague who turned and headed back to the apartment. Hawk stared at Mark but didn't comment. He winked to Jack who nodded.

"Let's hit the road," Jack said.

Larson headed toward the freeway on a course that would take them to New Mexico. The plan called for them to take turns driving and stop only for gas and meals. Jack wondered what Cassandra would select from the menus from the bar and grills along the route. There weren't too many vegetarians in those border towns.

Ricky sat as far away from Larson as possible and glared at him. When Larson didn't respond, he turned his attention to Cassandra and leered at her. She didn't seem to notice or care. Hawk's eyes were riveted on Cassandra, but Jack trusted his friend to keep quiet. Still, he knew Hawk realized he would probably never have another chance to talk with a real extraterrestrial.

Jack had questions of his own that Cassandra never had answered. She seemed to talk around some subjects without ever addressing them directly. He wondered whether it was part of the way she thought, the way her culture handled direct questions, or simply a way for her to avoid answering questions. He remembered his time in Japan when he had been part of a team questioning a Japanese terrorist and how frustrating it had been because the Japanese language and culture made it almost impossible to ask the suspect direct questions or for him to make any definitive admissions. *Maybe she deserves a pass*, he thought.

Cassandra seemed fixated on her mission. Still, he wondered what she meant by her remark that death was just another state. Could the dead on her world communicate with the living? She seemed totally indifferent to whether someone lived or died. If asked, he knew that Cassandra would have killed the SWAT team members without any feelings of remorse. She was a cold-blooded killer. Was she any different from the cold-blooded reptiles called the Draconians? Would her people kill humans

148

without any second thoughts if they wanted to take over the Earth?

Jack pondered those questions as well as others as they sped toward Dulce. After many hours of traveling, the van pulled up to a dusty bar and grill in a sleepy border town. Jack heard the music playing before he entered and realized it was a cowboy bar. *Bound to be lots of rednecks*, he thought. *Best to get in and out quickly before there's any trouble*. He looked over at Ricky and prayed his friend wouldn't start something.

They sat at a large table a few feet away from the bar. The ex-SEALS wolfed down hamburgers and drank beer while Cassandra and Hawk settled for cheese pizza and salads. Jack could feel unfriendly eyes on them. When Ricky turned and glared at several men who sat on stools at the bar, Jack recognized that look. Ricky was challenging them; they'd either rise to the challenge or back down. Either way Ricky would enjoy himself.

Cassandra excused herself and headed to the restroom. For a moment, Jack found himself wondering just how close to human she was when it came to her bodily functions, but he dismissed that idea and felt ashamed of himself. He noticed that the men at the bar had turned away so that they now faced the bar; they talked quietly while Ricky looked triumphant. A couple of them rose, said something to the bartender, and headed in the direction of the restrooms.

Jack realized after several minutes that Cassandra still hadn't returned and decided he better make sure she was okay. The men sitting at the bar stared at him as he passed, but they didn't say

149

anything. Few men challenged him, especially when he wore his SEAL T-shirt that accentuated the size of his biceps.

Jack turned a corner and saw something that made his blood run cold. Two men lay flat on their backs, apparently unconscious, while Cassandra stood nearby staring at them.

"What happened?" Jack demanded.

"They were waiting for me when I came out, and they said they wanted sex. When I said no, one put his hands on me."

Cassandra shrugged to indicate the logical consequences of what followed.

"Are they alive?"

Cassandra shook her head. "I just reacted. I didn't have time to think. I'm sorry."

Jack figured that the men's restroom at that place probably received far more business than the women's, so he dragged the bodies through the door marked WOMEN and balanced the men on commodes before closing the doors. *That should buy us some time*, he thought. He then put his hand on Cassandra's arm and led her back to the table. "Quick. Let's get out of here," he whispered.

"What happened?" Ricky said, his mouth still half full.

"Two guys attacked Cassandra and she offed them."

"I didn't hear any shots. What kind of weapon did she...? Oh, I get it," Ricky said and smirked. He moved his hands in a way that suggested a ninja using Kung Fu.

150

Milburn stared at the young woman. "These rednecks are liable to lock all of us up and throw away the key."

Jack reached for his wallet and put three twenty dollar bills on the table. "Let's move now," he said as he turned toward the door. The others followed him and piled back into the van. Larson gunned the engine and headed toward the highway.

"How much time before they find out?" Larson asked without turning his attention from the road.

"We probably have a couple of hours at best if we're lucky," Jack said.

"From now on, let's stick to take-out places," Larson said.

Chapter 18

"How long before we reach the New Mexico border?" Milburn asked as he turned his head to look behind them. The group had been traveling an hour, but they couldn't help glancing frequently at their side mirrors.

Jack studied the map in his lap. "It looks like around an hour more."

"Damn!" Larson cursed as he looked into his rearview mirror and saw the red flashing lights of a highway patrol car.

"He'll be radioing in that he's located us," Milburn said.

Cassandra reached into her bag and began turning the dial of a device that looked like a hair curler. She aimed it at the approaching car and turned to Jack. "He won't be able to communicate now. I've jammed all frequencies. He'll probably think he's in a dead zone."

"He can't use his cell phone?" Ricky said.

"Look behind you," Cassandra ordered. The men turned their heads and saw the car fading in the distance.

"Why'd he stop?" Milburn said.

"All his electrical systems are out," Cassandra said calmly and turned her attention to another device she'd taken from her bag. She ignored the looks from all the men.

Larson kept glancing into his rearview mirror. Finally he shook his head. He muttered to himself for several minutes before turning to Cassandra. "How come our electrical system didn't get fried?"

"It's directional," Cassandra said in an even tone. Jack wondered whether she really understood human body language.

"Guys, I haven't been completely straight with you. Cassandra does work for another government, but it's not Israel."

"Hell, we're not morons," Milburn said.

"No shit, Sherlock. I think Jack's honey isn't a real Earth girl," Ricky said.

"Is she one of those Dorks?" Larson said. His entire body tightened. Jack recognized the fight or flight response because he'd seen all his men enough when they were under duress.

"She's not a reptile, and she bleeds just like us. Her planet's an enemy of the Draconians."

"I'm from Androvia," Cassandra said as if that answered all their questions.

"How the hell do we know we can trust her?" Ricky said.

Jack understood him enough to know his male pride still hurt from having a female of whatever species handle him so effortlessly. "She's a combination scientist and warrior. She really does have the technology to give us cards that will get us through the Draconian checkpoint."

"I can think of at least one way that you can prove you're almost human," Ricky said.

Cassandra looked at him and then made a self-defense like motion with her hands. He jerked his legs and head away from her. His seatbelt and shoulder strap kept the rest of him immobile.

"She also has weapons we need. I'll vouch for her," Jack said.

"How do we know you're not lying now?" Larson said.

"What would be the point? Either you trust me enough now that you know she's an alien on our side or you don't. We need all of us to be successful. Every one of you is critical to our mission."

Ricky looked at Jack and then nodded. "Whatever she is, I'd rather have her on our side than against us."

Larson took a deep breath and let it slowly while staring at the road passed before him. He gripped the steering wheel tightly. "I knew she wasn't human. If you do that crinkling thing you do with your eyes when you stare at her and then tell me she's okay, I'm still in."

"Me too," Milburn said.

Jack looked at Hawk, and his friend smiled and gave him a thumbs- up. So, he squinted at Cassandra for a couple of minutes without speaking. The van was very quiet. Cassandra continued to work with the strange device in her lap. Jack marveled at how calm she remained.

"She's okay," he finally announced. Larson loosened his grip on the steering wheel and let another breath out slowly. Milburn laughed nervously while Ricky smiled.

"How long is that patrol car going to be out of service?" Larson asked. He spoke directly to Cassandra now and not through Jack.

"I think most of the car's electrical circuits are burned beyond repair."

"So we'll be in New Mexico and long gone before anyone finds him," Larson concluded.

"As long as we don't run into another hotshot cop who wants to stop us for speeding," Jack said. Larson looked sheepish and the car slowed. Jack read the speedometer and saw they were cruising now at 80 mph.

Chapter 19

Jack breathed a sigh of relief as the van crossed the New Mexico border and headed toward Dulce. "Welcome to New Mexico, home of rocks, sand, and alien reptiles who want to kill us!"

"All I see is desert. What's your planet like?" Hawk asked.

Jack saw his team turn toward Cassandra. He'd been wondering the same thing himself.

"It's not desert like this," she said.

"It's like trying to drag something out of a spy," Larson spat. "Come on, tell us what it's like."

Once again Jack wondered whether Cassandra was being deliberately evasive or she really didn't understand people. She was answering briefly but not volunteering anything.

"Tell us what you think we would notice about the place," Jack said.

"It's a much larger planet, and it's at the very edge of what your scientists call the Goldilocks zone that supports life. You would probably find it colder and much dimmer. The gravity is heavier there, so you might have trouble running or jumping. Over the centuries we've moved under domes or underground. Since our world is much older than yours, we really don't have mountains anymore. They're more like what you would call hills. We have water, of course, but no animals."

"No animals?" Milburn interrupted.

"No, they died out centuries ago."

"No birds?"

"No. On the positive side, we don't have insects either because they can't handle the cold."

"So why do the Draconians want your planet? What do you have of value?" Jack asked. The question had bothered him from the moment she said she wanted to be allies.

"They would like to get their hands on our technology. They have acquired most of their science through conquest since they are incapable of developing their own. We're the only civilization left anywhere near them with enough technology to arm Draco's enemies sufficiently to keep them from forcing everyone to bow before them."

"Do all the women look like you?" Ricky asked and licked his lips. Jack had seen the act enough that he'd grown very tired of it, but no one was perfect.

"Do all your men look alike?" Cassandra replied.

"Okay, good point," Ricky said. "How'd you get here? Where's your spaceship?"

"Spaceship? Very few worlds have spaceships."

"How did you get here from your planet?"

"I can't explain the technology, but it's almost instantaneous. It does require a lot of power at both ends, though."

"No way," Larson said.

"It's what we're just starting to learn about in physics. Think of beaming from one place to another in *Star Trek*," Hawk added.

"Are your bodies like ours?" Milburn said.

"Pretty much. We tend to be smaller than your people because we're vegetarians. Jack will vouch that I'm pretty much like any Earth girl."

"Yeah, except she can kill you with her bare hands," Ricky added. Larson drove slowly down Dulce's dusty main street. "My kind of town," Ricky said as he laughed and pointed to all the pickup trucks with gun racks.

"Notice the stickers on their windshields," Jack added.

"They probably only get you past the first security checkpoint at the main gate," Milburn said.

"There's a hidden entrance outside of this town," Cassandra said. When Jack gave her a puzzled look, she pulled a piece of paper out of her bag and handed it to him.

"These are GPS coordinates?"

"Yes, you should be able to type them into your navigation system."

"Anything else we need to know?" Jack said as he handed the paper over to Larson.

"I think we should eat and relax. It would be better to enter at night because they patrol the area with aircraft," Cassandra said.

Milburn's eyes bore into Cassandra. He turned to the other members of the team. "She's a keeper," he said.

"You'll all need warmer clothes." Cassandra looked at the men and frowned. "The temperature will drop very quickly once the sun goes down even though the Draconians keep the lower levels they control much warmer."

"They're really coldblooded like alligators or snakes?" Ricky asked.

"Yes, and they enjoy killing, particularly anything warm blooded, and they're very good at it." Her matter-of-fact tone made what she said even more chilling.

"Maybe that's why we all fear and hate reptiles. It seems to be bred into us," Hawk mused. "The *Bible* story about Eve and the snake is interesting. I think it goes back to a very early time when the Draconians first came to Earth." Ricky crossed himself.

"Maybe we owe them one for Eve," Larson said and smiled.

"You're not afraid of snakes, are you?" Milburn said as he turned in Cassandra's direction.

"No, just remember the story in your *Bible*. The snake lied to Eve.

The Draconians lie without any remorse or hesitation. Don't think twice about it when you have the chance to kill one because otherwise it might talk you out of it and then kill you."

"You know an awful lot about them," Ricky said.

"I've studied them for a very long time. They've killed many of my friends," Cassandra said.

"Have you killed any?" Milburn said.

"I've killed them, but they're not easy to kill." Cassandra spoke softly.

The men grew silent, lost on their own thoughts. Jack thought of the many missions he'd gone on with his team. It was always the same just before they deployed. He glanced over at Hawk and saw that his friend stared straight ahead. Only when he looked at Hawk's hands did he notice that his knuckles were white from gripping his seat belt so tightly. Jack realized he'd have to be careful where he put his friend once they were in the field. He couldn't trust him on the perimeter or with one of the heavy weapons.

The afternoon went by quickly. They found a fast food drive through and ordered. Hawk and Cassandra struggled, but eventually they found something they could eat. Larson parked the van off the main road, and the SEAL team concentrated on checking their weapons and organizing the equipment they'd take with them. Cassandra went through the various items in her bag while Hawk looked over her shoulder. He then looked in his bag and studied the device he constructed with Cassandra's help. As the sun began to set, the temperature began to drop sharply. The men had donned sweatshirts while Cassandra and Hawk put on jackets.

Larson looked at the GPS coordinates Cassandra had brought with her.

"You're positive this is right?"

"Yes, it's off a dirt road. There are some large trees near the spot where you can park and not be seen from the air."

Larson followed the directions given by the mechanical voice on his GPS system. Before long it directed him to turn down an unmarked dirt road that looked more like a path. Jack stuck his head out the window and studied the road as they drove slowly.

"There are some deep grooves. You can just see them because the last rain left some mud. It looks like some large trucks came this way not too long ago."

160

"Why here and not the main gate?" Hawk asked.

Jack shrugged, so Hawk looked at Cassandra.

"If you go this way, you can drive down a ramp. I think they designed it to make it easier to offload heavy equipment from a truck directly to the magnetic train. Whatever they deliver here is probably too large to fit in an elevator."

"Is the ramp guarded?" Milburn asked.

"Yes, by two guards. There's a checkpoint much further down where they require the special passes," Cassandra said.

"How do you know that?" Milburn said.

"It proves that my passes work, doesn't it?" Cassandra stared back at Milburn until he turned away.

"She's been here and gone down to the second level on a scouting mission," Jack said.

"I can't believe you're really an alien," Larson said. His voice reflected more excitement than fear.

"Anyone not born on this planet is an alien. I'm from a planet much like yours except we have been at war with the Draconians for over two hundred years. Jack can vouch that there's no difference between me and a human female, at least nothing important."

"I wish my chicas looked more like you," Ricky said with a smirk.

Cassandra pulled a white U.S. Government contractor sticker from her bag and handed it to Larson. "Put this on your front windshield."

"How did you get one?" Milburn said. He was studying Cassandra the way a group of eighth graders on a field trip to the zoo stare at snakes.

161

"Alien magic," Cassandra said with a straight face. Jack groaned. She recited the details like a first grader describing her day at school. "The last time I was here I took a picture of one on a truck when the driver was in a bar. When I got home, I used a basic photo editing program to make some changes and then I printed it."

"Is the sticker all you need to get past the two guards?" Milburn said.

"It should be, but I'll use my weapon if they become suspicious. It won't make any noise, so the guards at the next checkpoint won't respond."

"Do you put your phaser on stun or kill?" Hawk asked. Cassandra stared at him without any hint of comprehension. "It's an old television show called *Star Trek*," Larson said helpfully.

"Are you Mister Spock?" Cassandra said, finally breaking into a smile.

"You know about that stuff?" Larson asked.

"I've been here awhile, and I do have a television." Cassandra placed her weapon on her lap and covered it with a blanket. She pulled a cap low over her brow. Larson approached the checkpoint slowly. The guards stood rock still and studied the van. When one saw the sticker, he leaned over and read the details.

What all are you guys carrying?" the soldier said with a strong southern accent.

"Communications equipment," Cassandra said before the others could reply. The soldier nodded and then motioned the van to proceed.

"Why communications equipment?" Jack said.

"It's what the truck with the sticker I copied was carrying. I figured there might be some kind of

162

code corresponding to the numbers on the sticker. I didn't want to take a chance you might say something that would alert the guards."

The van slowly drove down the ramp. It opened into a very large, well-lit tunnel that far larger vehicles could travel without coming too close to the walls on either side. The tension among the men was contagious. Jack glanced at Cassandra and whistled in surprise. She had placed a carefully molded mask over her face. It provided her with a much darker complexion and a much broader nose. She pulled the cap even lower so only her eyes showed.

"Why the disguise now?" Jack asked.

"The Draconians would recognize my type and attack," she said. "Your type?" Hawk asked.

Cassandra seemed to be searching for the right words. "We're not as... diverse in our appearance as humans," she said and then gave a very human-like shrug.

"Remind me to visit your planet," Ricky said as Larson nodded.

"Have your cards ready. You'll have to step out of the van and be weighed, and then you'll have to place your cards in a slot for verification," Cassandra said.

"So, these guys are not really human?" Larson asked.

"They should be human. Anyone you meet past this checkpoint is liable to be a Draconian. They're all about Jack's size but with dark hair and dark eyes."

"But they look human, right?" Milburn said.

163

"If you wound them, their transponder will fail and they'll revert to their real appearance. You can't let it startle you and cause you to hesitate. You must keep shooting until you kill them."

"Where should we aim?" Milburn said.

"Their scales are so tough that one bullet won't even slow them down. Aim for their stomach or try to get a face shot. Their eyes aren't protected."

The men digested Cassandra's comments and remained silent as the van continued its slow progress. It turned a corner and came to a checkpoint with a gate that was down. Two armed guards stood with assault rifles aimed at the van while a third guard moved to the driver's side and looked into the van.

"You'll have to step out and go through the usual process," he said as he studied the boxes. Jack had covered the weapons with empty boxes at Cassandra's request.

The guard led Cassandra and the men to a machine that looked like one that did parking ticket validations. Cassandra stepped on a slightly raised platform directly in front of the machine and placed her card very confidently into the slot. The machine made a mechanical sound that resembled that of an electric pencil sharpener. After a couple of minutes, the machine spat out Cassandra's pass and a light glowed green. The guard nodded and motioned for Jack to follow Cassandra's example.

Each of the men in turn placed a pass into the machine and waited for the green light. Hawk came last. When the machine finally glowed green, the guard motioned for the group to get back in the van and continue.

"You'll have to leave everything at the next checkpoint because that's as far as your passes permit," one of the guards said.

"We'll be quick," Jack said.

The guard glared at Jack for a moment and then frowned. "You better be quick and zip your lips. You give those guards at the next checkpoint any lip, and I guarantee you won't be coming back my way. Those mean motherfuckers down there don't take any shit."

Larson drove the van down the ramp that banked downward at an increasingly sharp angle. Milburn peered out his window. "It's getting warmer. Can you feel it?"

"Nice and warm for alligators and snakes," Ricky said. He picked up an assault rifle and inspected it carefully.

"Don't use that yet. I'll handle the guards in a much quieter way," Cassandra said. She didn't seem to notice Ricky glaring at her.

"Ricky usually gives orders now rather than takes them," Jack said. He looked at Cassandra for some hint she understood him, but she ignored him. She clutched her tiny weapon in her lap.

The road seemed to stretch down forever. Jack monitored the time on his watch and saw it had only been ten minutes since they had passed the last checkpoint, even though it seemed to have been an eternity. He noticed his men were at high alert. Hawk's ragged breathing made him wonder if he'd been too quick to invite his friend to join them. Only Cassandra remained completely still. Anyone looking at her would think she was enjoying a vacation trip rather than facing almost certain death.

Despite himself and his feelings for her, Jack wondered if she really was warm blooded. *She'd been bruised, but had he actually ever seen any blood?*

The van turned a corner sharp enough to force Larson to jam his brakes. A checkpoint stood immediately in front of them, and Jack saw that the three guards standing by the gate were huge and wore uniforms signifying they were Draconians.

"Everyone out. Keep your hands where we can see them," the closest guard said in a deep gravelly voice. Larson climbed out of his driver's seat and opened the back door for Milburn. Jack caught a slight movement and saw Cassandra had twisted her weapon and tapped some kind of pattern into the indentations. Her finger tightened on the button.

The Draconian guards looked stunned. One started to say something, but he fell to the ground. The other two guards reached for their weapons, but whatever Cassandra did caused them to drop to the ground before they could fire. Almost like magic the human figures morphed into figures Jack knew he'd seen in the nightmares he had after reading some of Hawk's books about Dulce. He stared at the yellow eyes, long snouts, wide cheeks and bodies covered with scales.

"Are they dead?" Jack said.

"Yes, we'd better hide the bodies," Cassandra said calmly. Jack and Larson casually started to drag one of the creatures, but they discovered that the task required all their combined strength.

"They must weigh close to three hundred pounds," Larson whispered as he struggled with one limb. Ricky and Milburn struggled with the second

Draconian. Hawk reached down to grab a limb of the third guard but gave up. Jack and Larson returned and hauled the creature into the guardhouse and laid him down.

"How come we didn't feel it this time?" Jack said.

"I adjusted the frequency band far enough over so it's right in the middle of the Draconians' frequency. If I had to stun them, then you'd feel some of the effect."

"How busy are they down here?" Jack said.

"The traffic should be non-existent this late."

"Do they have to report in on a regular basis?"

"I think so, but I don't know for sure. We realized we couldn't get any further without more help, so we turned around once we delivered some equipment we took off a truck parked in downtown Dulce."

Jack groaned. "So we might find a reception committee in a few minutes when these guys fail to report that they're okay."

"Let's make every minute count," Milburn said. "We know from Hawk's books that people like Pete probably are down in level four. As soon as any Draconian spots us, we'll be in a firefight."

"The elevator is around that corner. Take everything you can carry because we won't be coming back this way," Cassandra said.

"We're leaving my van?" Larson said with mock concern.

"Didn't you listen when we went over the plan?" Jack said.

"I'm just joshing with the alien," Larson said.

"She has a name," Jack said.

Larson turned away and wouldn't meet his eyes. Cassandra pulled a strange looking tube from the back of the van while Hawk carefully placed his anti-magnetic contraption into his backpack so he could keep his hands free to hold his weapon. Jack filled his backpack with weapons from Ricky's arsenal. The men worked methodically and then signaled when they were ready. Cassandra led them through the gate and then toward a wall that was filled with strange looking symbols that resembled Egyptian hieroglyphics. Hawk stared at them with his mouth open until Jack jabbed him in the ribs and motioned for him to continue.

"Is that the Draconian language?" Hawk whispered.

"Yes, it says humans are being served for lunch on Tuesdays," Cassandra said.

The men stopped and stared at her. She smiled. "It says elevator to all levels in this direction."

"The humor doesn't translate," Milburn muttered.

"How come you can read Draconian?" Larson asked.

"How come you can read some Spanish? The Draconians control a big chunk of the universe. If you want to defeat them, you have to understand them. My people have studied them for centuries."

"Our cards won't work on that elevator, will they?" Jack said as they approached it.

"No, not for going down. I doubt these guards even had clearance to reach the fourth level. Only scientists and elite soldiers have that kind of clearance. I can fool the system enough to get us down to that level, but an alarm will sound when the

168

door opens because I don't have the names of any Draconian scientists authorized for that level. We must be ready to fire even before the door opens."

Cassandra took out a different looking pass from her pocket and stuck it in the elevator. As it approached, she motioned for Jack to raise his weapon. "There might be someone coming up," she said.

Jack aimed so he could fire while the door was opening, but he didn't see any figures. They climbed in and Cassandra studied the panel before pressing a symbol.

"Each level is far deeper. It will take a few minutes. I'll give you a warning just before we get there."

Jack motioned for his men to flatten themselves against both sides of the elevator, leaving most of the platform completely empty. Anyone taking a quick look at the opening elevator wouldn't see anything immediately. He looked at Hawk's face and smiled. "This beats putting makeup on stiffs, doesn't it?"

Hawk nodded and gripped his weapon even tighter. Cassandra watched the lights change on the panel as the elevator descended. There was absolutely no feeling of falling. Hawk looked at Cassandra and whispered something.

"Technology the Draconians took from the Lyrians when they conquered their world. We're almost there, and soon you'll hear an alarm. It's different than what you are used to hearing because of you will only be hearing a small part of its frequency," she whispered.

"Aim for the stomach, right?" Larson whispered.

"Yes, but you better put your weapons on auto because their scales can stop a single bullet," she said.

"Holy mother of God," Hawk whispered.

"God has nothing to do with these creatures," Cassandra whispered as she raised her weapon.

Chapter 20

The elevator began broadcasting a very high-pitched scream just as it opened. Two Draconian guards stood in front of the elevator, apparently waiting for entry. They heard the sound and began reaching for their weapons. Cassandra aimed at one soldier while Jack opened up on the second one. Both fell to the ground.

"This way. The sound of your weapon will bring many more of them," Cassandra said as she led them down a passage.

As Jack ran behind Cassandra, he saw what appeared to be small enclosures built into the wall. He realized they were cages containing men and women. They weren't completely human. Those differences were so stark that the men paused before continuing.

"The ones still human should be over in this direction," Cassandra whispered as she continued to move rapidly down the passageway with Hawk bringing up the rear. He glanced behind him and saw two Draconians with their weapons raised.

"Duck," he shouted.

Jack threw himself against one of the walls as he turned and fired. Something hot whizzed over his head. Larson had flattened himself on the other wall and was firing as well while he muttered to himself. Milburn, Hawk, and Cassandra had flattened themselves on the ground. When it became clear that the two Draconians were down, the men rose. Cassandra was already on her feet and moving down the passage.

"We owe you, man," Ricky muttered to Hawk, who smiled.

Jack was running closely behind Cassandra. "We just can't leave the people who are still alive down here," he said.

"The Draconians have already inoculated them with their DNA, and now it is too late to save them because their bodies will keep changing in a way we cannot fix," Cassandra said.

The group turned another corner and saw a group of armed Draconian soldiers who began firing their weapons. Jack motioned with his arm and his team dove around the corner so the wall would give them cover. The soldiers fired, and Jack saw part of their protective cover blown to bits.

"Might be a good time to use Carl," Ricky said as he reached in his backpack. He gripped the weapon in both hands, readied it, and fired as he stuck his head around the corner. The explosion rocked the building and knocked Ricky and the others off their feet. Jack peered around the corner.

"All clear. I think you got all of them," he said. Jack kept his finger wrapped around his trigger as he slowly approached the debris. Bodies and debris lay everywhere. Milburn stared at the pile of bodies with scales and snouts.

"Every Draconian within five miles is going to be heading this way," Larson said as Ricky glared at him.

"Just be glad we didn't have to fight them with your little pee shooter," Ricky said.

"Your friend should be in the holding cells just ahead," Cassandra said. She stepped ahead of Jack and took the point much to his surprise. He realized she played by a different set of rules and didn't understand how his team worked. He followed her closely, but turned to Hawk.

"Keep checking behind you every couple of minutes. I don't want anyone sneaking up on us," he said. Hawk nodded.

Cassandra pointed to a row of glass-enclosed rooms. "Your friend should be here. If he's not, then we're too late."

Jack passed a woman who lay naked huddled on the floor in a fetal position. He passed a man who lay on the floor amid puddles of what looked like blood. Purple bruises covered his face.

Ricky paused and looked at the man and nodded approvingly. "Looks like he fought them," he said.

"It didn't do him much good," Hawk whispered.

Ricky turned and sneered at the mortician. "Only cowards give up without a fight," he said.

Hawk started to say something but decided against it. He turned to look behind him and shrugged. Ricky stared at Hawk but then turned his attention back to the front. Jack smiled and pointed to a cell. A man lay on the floor with a large white bandage covering part of his head.

"We found Pete. I can see that he's breathing, but I don't know what kind of shape he's in," Jack said. He raised his weapon and fired through the glass but well above the figure on the floor. Instead of shattering, the wall just seemed to absorb the bullets. He looked questioningly at Cassandra.

"It's not glass. You can't break it by shooting since the material is harder than your bullets."

"How do we break it then?" Jack's voice revealed his exasperation.

Cassandra studied her weapon and then began tapping on it. Jack had never studied the weapon that closely, but now he noticed that a tiny set of raised dots must serve as an instrument panel.

She lifted her weapon and fired it at the window. Nothing seemed to happen although Jack found himself staggering because everything around him began spinning around. When she stopped firing at the window, he suddenly felt better. He looked up at the window and noticed no change. Then he saw a tiny crack on one corner. The crack seemed to widen and deepen until it ran the full length of the window. When a number of other cracks appeared, she motioned to Ricky, and he slammed his weapon against the window. It crumbled rather than shattered. Pieces seemed to break into still smaller pieces before falling to the ground. Jack already was inside the room, bending over his friend.

Larson opened his backpack and pulled out a first aid kit. He handed a small package to Jack, who opened it and lifted what looked like a piece of cotton to his friend's nose. He held it there until the man started coughing. His eyes opened slowly, and he stared at Jack. He looked over Jack's shoulder and saw the others.

"I knew you guys would come for me!" "Can you walk? We have to get out of here!" Jack said.

Moon rose with some assistance. He shook his head the way a dog shakes off water when coming out of a pool. "I can walk. If you have another rifle, I'd be obliged."

174

Ricky handed a weapon to Moon, who checked to make sure it was loaded.

"We don't have much time," Jack said.

"We need to go this way," Cassandra said as he began walking down a corridor to the right of them.

"The plan says we get to the trains and get out of here. I thought they were to the left," Jack said.

"The trains are to the left. There is something else we must do. The Draconian quantum trans-dimensional generator is over here. We need to destroy it to keep the Draconians from sending reinforcements."

Jack looked at Cassandra and shook his head. "Why didn't you bring that up earlier? We probably have already attracted every Draconian in five miles. Why take a chance?"

"If you're not brave enough, go to the trains and I will follow. I can do this by myself."

It's not a question of brave enough. I'm not sure what your deal is. I'm beginning to wonder if we can trust you," Jack said.

Cassandra began moving down the passage. She spoke without looking back. "If you don't keep more Draconians from coming here, eventually they will take over your world and millions of your people will die."

Jack looked at his friends and saw all of them including Hawk nodding. He shrugged and motioned for them to follow him as he moved quickly to catch up with Cassandra. She reached a dead end as the path turned to the right. Jack reached into his pocket and pulled out a grenade because he had the same feeling in his gut that he always got just before something terrible happened.

He saw Cassandra raise her weapon as she stuck her head around the corner. He felt slightly dizzy and saw Cassandra fall to the ground. He dragged her back behind the wall and saw blood pouring from her shoulder.

Jack pulled the pin as he turned the corner and threw the grenade. He dove back to safety, but he caught a glimpse behind the crowd of a large piece of equipment that seemed to cover one entire wall.

Chapter 21

Jack held the antiseptic wipe tightly against Cassandra's shoulder. The blood slowed just enough for him to wrap a compression bandage tightly around the wound. Larson glanced at the wound.

"I guess she was telling the truth when she said that she bleeds like us," he said.

Cassandra smiled weakly and rose to her feet with Jack's help. "We should leave now and head that way," she said and pointed down a long corridor.

"Hawk, stay at the rear and shout if you see anyone behind us," Jack said.

The group moved quickly down the hollowed out passageway. There were no signs, no decorations; they only saw blank walls. Jack saw a Draconian weapon on the ground similar to the one Cassandra held. He picked it up and stuffed it in his pocket. He probably would need all the firepower he could carry.

"They're not much for making stuff pretty," Milburn muttered.

"They have no art, no music, and no culture because they're a race of warriors that only cares about conquering or dying bravely. They kill their children if they show any weakness," Cassandra added.

Larson gripped his rifle tighter and glanced behind him. Jack kept one hand on Cassandra's arm to help prop her up and thanked God she was so light. She stopped suddenly and raised her arm. The men froze.

"The tracks are right around this corner. I see two Draconians waiting. Let me handle them, and then let's go." Cassandra stepped around the corner and fired her weapon. All the men watched her in action, and Ricky nodded with appreciation.

"Wherever she's from, they train them real good. She hasn't missed once."

Cassandra waved her arm and the men hurried to follow. Hawk took one look back and froze. "Duck! They're coming," he said. Just as they hit the ground, a burst of what felt like hot air streamed over their heads. Ricky turned and fired his Carl Gustav. The sound almost deafened them, but the explosion cleared the passageway of the Draconians.

"The train's here!" Milburn shouted.

Jack looked up, surprised because he hadn't heard any sound. A large brown colored vehicle shaped like a gigantic bullet pulled up and stopped. Cassandra motioned and the men followed her. She placed a hand on a door and it opened silently. The men entered. They saw benches inside with very deep depressions.

"It looks empty. What about the driver?" Milburn said.

"No driver. Everything's programmed from here, depending on which station you need," Cassandra said.

Larson sat, but immediately he began squirming as he moved forward and then backward in the seat.

"It's made to fit the Draconians," Cassandra said. She walked to a wall containing a sign in the Draconian language and studied it before nodding.

"It's going in the direction we want. What we don't want is another train to follow us."

Hawk smiled and took out the strange looking contraption he had carried with him. He pointed in the direction where the train had come and pressed a lever. Nothing seemed to happen, but Cassandra's lips cracked into a small smile.

"I can tell it worked. Let's go now." She looked below the sign she had read and placed her hand over a series of buttons. She moved her hand over them without actually touching them. Suddenly the train began to move. While there wasn't any feeling of movement, the scenery changed as the train left the station. Soon they saw nothing but blackness.

"What if there's a reception party waiting at the next station?" Jack said.

"I bypassed the intermediate stops. We'll be traveling at least thirty minutes until we reach the last station. I'm sure guards will be waiting for us there, but you'll understand later why they won't want to use heavy weapons on us," she said.

The group sat silently while the only evidence of the train's rapid movement were the tunnel's markers that they saw fly by them. Suddenly the men began grabbing their heads in anguish. Jack saw Cassandra appear to lose consciousness. He felt a stab of pain in his head and then heard a voice in his head. Surprisingly, it spoke in English.

He looked in the direction of the car that housed the engine and saw a door open and a figure, distinctly alien, move toward them. The alien resembled the popular conception of what an alien should look like. The small figure was gray with huge dark eyes that lacked an iris. It wore what looked like a silver colored uniform.

"You will do exactly what I tell you. The pain you now feel is nothing compared to the pain I can inflict on you."

Jack put his hand on his forehead even though he knew the gesture wouldn't make the stabbing pain in his head go away. His team appeared to be in far more pain than he was. Hawk was whimpering like a small child while Larson's face had turned white. Cassandra lay on the floor, but Jack saw that her body was quivering, apparently in pain. He wondered why he could still function.

Jack heard the alien's voice again. "You are now prisoners of the Draconian Alliance. You will be turned over to a Draconian warrior when this vehicle stops."

The alien looked dispassionately at Cassandra's body and then focused his eyes on her. She began shaking uncontrollably as if she were convulsing. Jack realized her body couldn't take too much more of that level of pain. He moved his right hand closer to his pocket, trying to be as inconspicuous as possible.

I'm almost there, he thought. At that moment the alien looked directly at him as if he had read his thoughts. He turned his eyes on him, and Jack's headache grew more severe. The pounding in his head increased until he felt he would pass out.

"You will not reach for the weapon," the voice in his head said.

Jack felt his resolve weaken as the pain intensified. The pain reminded him of the sessions he had with his shrink. He turned his mind to his mantra and focused on it with all his remaining will. Gradually the pain in his head began to dissipate. He thrust his hand in his pocket and pulled out the weapon, pointed it at the alien and pushed the button.

Nothing seemed to happen for a couple of seconds although the air around the alien seemed to waver. Suddenly the alien exploded, and its body seemed to dissolve before Jack's eyes.

Jack's headache went away, and his men seemed to be recovering rapidly. He reached over and picked up Cassandra and placed her on a seat by his side. He held her and studied her face. Gradually her color returned, and he saw her eyes flicker. They opened, and Jack saw that she recognized him.

"You saved us! The Traveler would have turned us over to his masters," she said in a voice that sounded exultant.

"You were strong enough to resist the Traveler's power of mind. I have never heard of anyone with the mental strength to be able to do that."

Jack saw his men now had all recovered. They stared at him as if he weren't human.

"How *did* you keep that headache from crippling you?" Larson said.

Jack had already asked himself the same question. "I don't know. I remembered how my shrink taught me to meditate whenever I got a bad headache. It worked. I did feel pain, but it probably wasn't nearly as bad as what you guys felt."

"Are there any more of those little buggers around?" Milburn said.

181

"There should be many more of them at our destination," Cassandra said.

Chapter 22

"How many of them are there here on Earth?" Larson said.

"The Travelers? I imagine a few hundred. They perform procedures on the people they abduct and assist the Draconians."

"They give me the creeps. What about the Draconians? How many do you think are here on Earth?" "Probably thousands, but they can't reproduce on this planet.

That's why it was so important to knock out their connection to their home planet."

"Our government is in on this. They're liable to come after us with everything they have once they hear what happened down here," Jack said.

"The treaty will be broken now that the Draconians have no way to send the heavy metals to their home planet. I think your government has more to worry about with the Draconians now than with us. They'll probably try to consolidate their territory."

"How long do they live?" Larson said

"Around thirty of your years. The gravity is heavier on this planet than on Draco, so it takes a toll on their hearts because of their size."

"That gives them plenty of time to do damage down here before they die out," Jack said.

"Most don't have that much time left since they send older, more elite troops here. Still, everyone we kill is one less to worry about."

Jack looked at Cassandra who talked so calmly in a way that sounded like dialog in a bad science fiction movie. "I'm not so sure that word will trickle down from the top that we're suddenly the good guys."

"I can get all of us back to San Diego, and then you can decide what you want to do," Cassandra said.

The tunnel's blackness broke occasionally as they neared well-lit stations, but the train continued at its same pace. Jack caught a glimpse of Draconians waiting at some of the stations. They took a step or two toward the train and then moved back quickly when they realized it wasn't going to stop.

Jack glanced at his watch and saw they should be approaching their final stop. He looked at Cassandra, who nodded.

"Be ready with your weapons," she said.

The train slowed beside a well-lit platform where Jack saw several guards looking in their direction. Cassandra calibrated her weapon and fired just as the door opened. The Draconians fell to the ground. Jack saw that some human looking figures dressed in suits appeared to be unarmed; they dove for cover when the shooting started.

"Who are they?"

"Your government's people. They're not allowed to carry weapons down here," Cassandra said. She dialed her weapon and then fired in their direction. Jack felt a little dizzy as the men fell to the ground.

"You didn't kill them, did you?" he said.

"No, I know your feelings about killing innocent people. They'll be okay. We have to move quickly now."

184

Cassandra led the men to an elevator where Jack's eyes grew wider as he saw that while the door contained directions in the Draconian language, the interior contained English directions as well. She pressed a button.

Jack saw the elevator's doors close, but it made no noise as it rose. He couldn't feel any movement, even though he saw the illuminated numbers change.

"It will stop soon. Try to stay out of sight and keep your weapons ready," she said.

The men flattened themselves against the walls. Jack stood next to Cassandra. He noticed that she wasn't even breathing hard. She might just as well have gone for a day in the park.

The door suddenly began to open. Jack saw a well-lit corridor and a sign in English that said *Immigration this way*.

"You've got to be kidding," he said.

"Your government tries to keep track of the Draconians as well as other ...visitors."

"Including your kind?" Jack said.

"No, we tried to approach your government once, but they threatened us. The Draconians already had convinced them that we were their enemy."

"So what do we do at Immigration?"

Cassandra pulled a strange looking device from her backpack. It resembled a large syringe. "I've studied the designs for this building. It's very late, so no one really expects us at this time."

She led them to a locked door, pointed her small weapon at it, and then pulled it open. She waved for them to follow her. Soon they came to another locked door. Instead of forcing the door open, she pointed at a nearby wall with her syringe-like device and slowly moved the plunger inward. The wall seemed to vibrate and then it began to crumble. Cassandra kept moving the device inward until a large hole stood where the wall had been.

"Follow me," she said.

The men walked through the hole. Jack could see bright lights in front of them.

"Keep only the guns you can hide," she said.

The men dropped their rifles and other assault weapons and followed the small woman. She stepped out of the wall. Each man looked around as he emerged.

"It looks like an airport terminal," Milburn said.

"It is. This section is officially closed for construction, but it never will reopen. If we walk to the left, we'll come to the main terminal."

"Where the hell are we?" Ricky said.

"Welcome to the Denver International Airport," Cassandra said.

Chapter 23

Larson saw a potted plant and started to ditch his weapon in it. "Don't," Cassandra said. She took out several pieces of silvery cloth from her backpack and distributed them to the men. She motioned for the others to follow her example as she wrapped her weapon with the cloth and placed the bundle back in her backpack.

"Aren't you afraid the x-ray machine will spot it?" Jack said.

"No, this material will reflect back into the machine. It will look as if nothing's there." Cassandra rummaged through her bag again and then began dispensing cards to the men. Ricky looked at his and laughed. "Robert Johnson. Could you have made me any more white bread?"

Jack studied his new California driver's license. It looked perfect. "More alien technology?"

"Nothing you can't buy at Office Depot," Cassandra replied and smiled. She put her hand on Jack's arm. "I've made us a married couple. I hope that's okay with you."

Jack gave her a quick hug before looking at his men. "Congratulate me, guys. We're married now."

"Usually the honeymoon comes after," Larson said.

"He's just jealous," Milburn said.

Cassandra pulled a credit card from her pocket. Larson glanced at it over her shoulder and shook his head. "You have Visa where you come from?"

"It's easy technology to fool," she said.

Jack watched Cassandra hand the card to a woman at the Southwest Airlines counter as he explained she would be paying for the entire group. *Alien hackers. What would the credit card companies say if they knew that aliens considered their best security to be a breeze to beat?*

The group went through the Southwest Airlines security line. They could still catch the last flight to San Diego. Jack held his breath as their backpacks went through the security conveyor belt. One TSA agent studied his screen and then pressed a button for the backpacks to continue to where the group waited to collect them. Jack watched Cassandra pick up her bag and proceed calmly toward the gate. *She was one cool operator! Imagine what a group of warriors like her could do? Even a well-trained SEAL team wouldn't be a match. There probably wasn't any defense for some of that Kung Fu stuff she did. Her weapons were far superior, and she never missed when she fired.*

The flight was uneventful. Jack and Cassandra sat close together as anyone would assume a married couple would do. She leaned her head against his shoulder and fell asleep. Jack saw that the compression bandage he had placed on her wound was holding. Her regular breathing convinced him she really was asleep. He studied her face and saw that the purple bruise, now almost healed, didn't detract from her perfect features. She seemed so vulnerable while sleeping. Still, Jack had seen her in action and now knew that she really was a warrior. Her marksmanship had been uncanny, as had her courage under fire.

Who could stop an army of aliens like her? Cassandra's companion, Mark or whatever his name is, what exactly was he doing? He wondered about her real mission. She'd blown up the gateway so the Draconians couldn't send reinforcements. Now what? How did she get here? What about that woman he'd seen who looked exactly like her? How many others like her were in the city?

Cassandra awoke as the plane went into its final descent. She opened her eyes and studied Jack. Her eyes seemed particularly penetrating in the dimly lit cabin.

"Jack, I think you're even more special than you think. You never showed fear. Some men probably would have left me when I was wounded. I knew you'd carry me if I couldn't continue."

"Maybe we can give ourselves a chance now that you've destroyed the gateway. I'd really like to feel there are no secrets between us," Jack said.

"I don't see any reasons for us to have secrets now," Cassandra said. She put her small hand within Jack's and squeezed it with surprising strength.

Using her phony ID and a credit card with the same name on it, Cassandra rented a van. She handed the keys to Jack with a smile. "I never learned to drive. They said husbands could drive if the wife's name is on the rental agreement."

Jack drove toward the mortuary. He kept stealing glances of Cassandra, who dozed next to him. She had the ability to relax completely almost instantly; she probably developed that trait in order to maximize her energy for when she needed it. He knew so little about her and her world. *How did people on Androvia get around if there weren't any cars?*

189

"Just drop me at the Greyhound depot," Pete said.

"Are you up for it? Maybe you should stay a day or two with us?" Jack said.

"I'm probably a lot safer leaving town right now. You guys are the ones who have to watch your backs."

The men embraced Pete. Jack hated to let go because he feared he would never see his friend again. Finally he released him and watched him turn and enter the Greyhound office. Cassandra approached him and placed something in his hand and whispered in his ear. He smiled and shook her hand.

"Next stop is the mortuary," Jack said.

"They're probably watching for any credit card transactions that have our names on them," Milburn said.

"I thought of that," Cassandra said and reached into her bag. She began distributing phony Visa cards with names on them that matched the identities of the IDs she already had handed out.

"You can work for me anytime," Ricky said as he admired his new card. "How long before these aren't any good?"

"The new billing cycle just started. You should be able to use these for the next three weeks."

Larson studied his card and whistled. "It's like found money. I'm getting me some cool stuff!"

"Sorry to ruin your fun, but the cards are linked to phony addresses. Your government has programs that match up names and addresses," she added.

"So transportation and food and hotels?" Larson said.

190

"They're all fine. Each of you has about twenty thousand dollars of credit."

The mortuary's lights were out as Jack passed it on the way to Hawk's house. The men climbed out, gathered their bags and shook hands before heading to their cars or trucks.

"Stay here until you find somewhere else," Hawk offered.

"I'll drop Cassandra off and come back," Jack said. On an impulse, he removed his gun from his bag and stuck it in his pocket. Cassandra looked at him and followed his example.

"Better safe than sorry," he said as he wondered whether anyone had recorded Cassandra's GPS coordinates when they had the tracker on his car.

"Cassandra's welcome to stay here as long as she wants. There's so many questions I want to ask her," Hawk said with obvious disappointment.

"I need to get back. My work with Mark is not finished." Cassandra turned to Jack. "You know where I live now, and I know where you are staying." She recited her cell phone number and Jack wrote it on the back of his airline receipt.

Cassandra moved closer to Jack as he drove her home. She laid her head against his shoulder. "It's very different to have someone who cares about me," she said.

"I do. Have I broken through your Androvian reserve yet? Do you have feelings like we do?"

"We have feelings. I do feel very close to you, and I care about you. I've never said that to anyone else."

Jack felt tears in his eyes, but he made no effort to brush them aside. "I'll walk you to the door," he

191

said as he parked at the far end of the lot, the only vacant parking spot in Cassandra's apartment complex.

He felt Cassandra slump into his arms. He realized he should do a 180-degree survey before proceeding, but that would mean releasing her. He wasn't ready for that yet. He smelled the sweet fragrance of her hair and felt her warm body close to his, as time seemed to stop. Jack took a deep breath, gave her a final hug, and then he slowly let her go. Cassandra adjusted the backpack on her shoulders and stood on her toes as she kissed him softly on his lips.

"I could get used to living here," she said. "Do you have to go back?" Cassandra's face clouded. "The project is very critical for my people. I told you I was a scientist as well as a warrior, and I have to finish my research and take the results back to my planet."

"After that?"

She shrugged in a very human way. "I don't know. I'll come back to you if they let me. Perhaps with the Draconian treaty no longer possible, your government will consider letting us come and go freely."

"Well then, let's hope that happens; meanwhile, we can be together. Maybe you could move in with me."

Cassandra brightened. "That's a wonderful idea!"

They held hands as they moved slowly toward her apartment. Suddenly, Jack saw a shadow out of the corner of his eye and his instincts kicked in. He shoved Cassandra behind a car and dove for cover.

Something hot passed over his head. He glanced at Cassandra and saw that she had a weapon in her hand. He pulled out his own as well.

"This car won't be enough protection," she said.

Jack saw that whoever fired at them was hidden in the shadows. "I'm going to move behind those cars and try to work around them. Maybe you can distract him," he said. Cassandra nodded, but clearly all of her attention was on the spot where their assailant had last fired.

Jack moved cautiously behind the parked cars, keeping as low as possible. He saw a car near their attacker burst into flames. He heard an explosion and saw that much of the car behind which Cassandra hid also was now burning. He prayed she was okay and told himself she was too good a warrior to stay very long in one spot.

Jack moved silently and quickly in the direction of his attacker. He saw a tree trunk explode and realized Cassandra must be shooting at someone hidden behind it. He took that as an invitation to run across an open space and then dive behind a van. He opened the door slightly to provide even more protection. Suddenly the windshield exploded and sent glass in all directions. He crawled down the row of cars. He felt something warm rolling across his face and touched it with his hand. He looked down and saw his hand covered with blood. The flying glass must have opened the wound. He ignored it and moved in the direction where Cassandra had fired.

"Over there," she whispered. Jack looked in the direction of her voice and saw a figure pointing toward a black SUV. *Of course, the place offering the most protection*, he thought.

Jack moved toward the SUV, careful to keep low so that parked cars kept their attacker from having a clear view. Cassandra must have seen him because she stepped out from behind a car to offer him some protective fire.

Just as she revealed herself, the figure behind the SUV fired. He didn't bother to stand up. His weapon was powerful enough for him to fire through the SUV's door, Jack realized. Then he saw Cassandra's body on the asphalt where she lay motionless.

***

Jack knew that even if she had survived the blast, Cassandra would not be able to survive another shot. He half stood and darted behind a car separated only a few feet from the SUV. When the figure rose to finish the job, Jack covered the distance in a few strides and slammed his shoulder firmly in the man's back. They fell to the ground and the weapon slid under a car.

Jack clung to the large figure but felt his grip slipping. The man turned and Jack realized that it was Scarpo, who smiled.

"Now I can finish it, and I won't have to hold back," he said.

"You're a damned Draconian," Jack said.

"I'm a warrior who has forgotten more about fighting than you'll ever know. I'm going to enjoy this," Scarpo snarled.

The two men battled on even terms for a few minutes, but Jack realized Scarpo had more stamina, and he felt himself weakening. "You'd never make

194

it out of our survival school," Scarpo said as his fist landed on Jack's cheek. The force pushed him back against a car. The alien threw himself on top of Jack and placed both hands on Jack's neck and began squeezing. Jack clawed at Scarpo, but it was useless. He began to feel the life drain out of him. "You never did figure out what your girlfriend is, did you? Now it's too late."

Jack's hands fell to his side. His right hand lay slightly underneath the car. He felt something hard and realized what it was; meanwhile Scarpo's hands tightened even more. With his last bit of energy Jack grabbed the weapon and moved his arm slowly from under the car. It seemed to take forever. He raised it toward the monstrous figure and pressed the button.

Nothing seemed to happen at first. Then Jack felt Scarpo's hands loosen and finally drop away from his neck. The alien's face seemed to dissolve as he was flung off Jack. The headless figure morphed into a hideous Draconian.

Jack gasped for breath and then he remembered Cassandra. He struggled to his feet and staggered to where she lay. He gathered himself and then reached down and lifted the slight figure into his arms. Her breathing was ragged, and he saw blood pouring from a wound on her side. He lifted her and ran toward her apartment while praying the entire time that Mark would have some kind of alien medicine that could save her.

Chapter 24

Jack pounded on the door; he heard movement inside and then Mark finally opened it and stared at the slight figure in his arms.

"She's been shot. You've got to help!"

"Put her on the sofa," Mark said. He spoke calmly, almost too calmly as far as Jack was concerned.

Jack placed her down gently and saw that Cassandra's blouse was covered in blood. *Yes, Ricky, she really does bleed like us,* he thought.

He watched as the alien bent over Cassandra and placed what looked like a saltshaker over the wound. He saw something flash and realized Mark was cauterizing it. The blood stopped, but Cassandra's face was white, and now her breaths came in gasps.

"She's lost too much blood," Mark said.

"Let's give her a transfusion. You can use my blood if you need it."

"You don't understand. My blood will not help her now and your human blood would be toxic. There's nothing I can do."

"You can't just let her die! There has to be something you can do. Can't you send her back to where you came from? You must have hospitals there!"

Mark shook his head. "That won't work. She couldn't survive the trip; she has very little time left even with her enhanced processes."

"What do you mean?" The words meant nothing to Jack.

"I can't explain. I don't have the words. She will be fine." "How can you say that? She's not going to be fine. You just told me she's dying!" Mark's facial expression didn't change. He looked down at Cassandra.

Jack noticed her breathing had stopped. He reached down to give her mouth-to-mouth, but Mark put a hand on his shoulder to stop him.

"She's dead. There really is nothing you can do."

"You don't seem that concerned. What did you mean everything's fine?"

"She is fine now. If you don't believe me, you can go where she is and ask her yourself."

Time stopped for Jack. He stared at the alien while he tried to digest his words.

"You're asking me if I want to die in order to see Cassandra?"

The alien shook his head, but he did so as if the gesture wasn't very natural for him. "You will be able to talk with her, but you will also be able to come back here. This is where you belong. It is not your time yet."

Jack studied the alien. *What did he really know about him? Could he trust him?* He weighed all that against the possibility of seeing Cassandra again and realized it wasn't much of a decision.

"What do I have to do?"

"Come back in one hour. I must send Cassandra's body back for disposal first. Then I will prepare what is necessary for your trip."

Jack realized he really didn't have any place to go. He thought of going back to Hawk's place, but didn't want to put his friend in any more danger

197

than necessary. He drove to a neighborhood bar where everyone's eyes were glued to the local Padre game that had gone into extra innings. He stared at the screen but realized he didn't care. It seemed trivial. Humans had debated about the nature of death for centuries; soon he'd know the answer, at least when it came to aliens from Androvia. He thought about some of the myths he'd studied in school where great warriors went after death to a place where they continued to hunt and fight forever. If such a place existed, then a warrior such as Cassandra might feel very comfortable there. He thought of her actions at Dulce and marveled once again at her lightening like reflexes; maybe the Androvians bred warriors selectively for centuries and Cassandra was the result.

He sipped a beer and watched the crowd. He'd placed his back against a wall and remained on high alert although nobody in the room looked like CIA or Navy Intelligence. There always was something about their cold dead eyes that gave them away. He contrasted that with the vitality he'd always seen in Cassandra's eyes. What did he want to say to her? Would he go to her after death? He thought of all the religious school classes he'd had. Nothing really prepared him for what he was about to do.

Jack glanced at his watch and saw it was time. He drove back to the aliens' apartment. This time he surveyed the parking lot very carefully before knocking on the door. Mark waved him in.

"I'm ready to proceed," the alien said.

Jack asked himself what bothered him about this creature and then realized it was the monotone with which he spoke. He sounded like a robot reciting English rather than a foreigner. Cassandra's slight accent had been charming.

He sat on the sofa and watched as the alien left the room briefly. Once again, he noted the whining sound coming from the closet. *Whatever equipment was in there, it must be generating a lot of power to make that kind of racket.* Soon the alien returned with what looked like a test tube filled with an amber-colored liquid.

"You must drink all of this. We've never given it to a human, but our systems are similar enough so that it should not harm you," the alien said in his monotone.

"That's reassuring. How long will this take?"

"Your sense of time will be very different, so time in your human sense really is meaningless. I will stay here with you until you return."

Jack took the test tube and stared at it. Somehow it seemed alive. He remembered stories he'd heard about the wild 1960s when drugs were plentiful and how many hippies had taken "trips" with LSD and claimed they saw God. Well, if he were going to see God, he had some questions for him including why so many good men he'd served with had died for no good reason. He lifted the test tube to his lips and began drinking.

Jack forced the foul tasting liquid down his throat. As he did so, he saw the alien's features change as they became almost transparent. He felt the room spin around and collapsed. He lay there very still.

He saw what looked like a large tunnel in front of where he stood. As he entered it, he saw the sides begin to spin around. They spun so fast he began to

199

feel dizzy. The tunnel seemed to go on forever, but in the far distance he began to see a bright light.

He's killed me. There's the bright light everyone who's had a near-death experience always mentions, Jack thought without any fear. He made the observation as casually as he if he were commenting on the weather.

It hadn't been a bad life; of course there were things to regret.

Jack finally became aware that he was approaching the light and that his rate of speed was slowing. He came to a dead stop just as the tunnel ended in blinding light. He stepped into the light and blinked his eyes and waited while they adjusted. He saw millions of pulsing lights yet somehow he knew they were far more than mere lights. He sensed he needed to move in the direction of the lights and realized he had begun floating toward them. He felt weightless.

No angels. No heavenly choir, but then again no Satan and no hell fire,

Jack thought. There was light everywhere but no sun or moon. He observed patterns of lights that seem to group together. They moved in complex patterns. He saw one light blink out and then another. He observed other lights suddenly appear. The light patterns became more and more complex as he moved among them. He sensed where he had to go.

He came upon a light that seemed somehow familiar. Suddenly he recognized the voice that spoke in his head.

"Jack, what are you doing here? You don't belong!"

He recognized Cassandra's voice. The light began to take shape and soon he saw it assume Cassandra's shape.

"Where am I? Are we both dead?"

"No, I told you it was complicated. I can tell that you don't belong here. You're in another dimension where our spiritual essence awaits its next incarnation. That's about the best I can do."

"I miss you. I'm so damned sorry I didn't take out Scarpo before he got to you."

"It doesn't matter. Do you see the pattern of lights around you? We're all part of a very complex pattern with lessons to learn each time."

Jack studied Cassandra and thought he detected a smile. "Maybe in my next incarnation I'll learn to duck."

"Is there any way I can touch you?"

"Come closer."

Jack approached the figure and then felt it wrap around him. "It's like we're one," he whispered.

Cassandra's voice echoed in his head. "We are, but this can't last. My colleague must have given you the inter-dimensional potion even though it probably would kill most humans. It will wear off before very long. You are so much luckier than you could possibly know. You have so much and we have been given so little."

Jack clung to the pulsating figure until he felt it start to pull away. "Will I come back here when I die?" he asked.

Cassandra's words came softly from the pulsating light. "No, this is not your place. We have different fates. You probably will go somewhere similar but a place reserved for your kind."

"Who makes the rules? Is there anyone I can talk to?"

Cassandra's voice was much weaker now and barely audible. "Humans have so little patience with rules. My people say this dimension has always existed. We are far more advanced in science, but even we cannot create life although I wish we could. Whoever made the rules must have a strange sense of humor because the rules for Androvia are very unfair."

Jack stared at the figure and felt himself moving backward toward the tunnel. He tried to resist. They had not even had time to say goodbye. The tunnel seemed to suck him in and propel him at such speed that he felt dizzy.

Jack seemed to exist in the darkness forever, but slowly he felt himself climbing out of the tunnel. He heard a loud whining sound and recognized something green. He realized it was the sofa on which he lay. He tentatively raised an arm and stared at it as if he belonged to someone else. His strength was gradually returning. He became aware of the alien studying him dispassionately.

"Are you feeling better?"

"I'll...be okay. Is it possible to go back and maybe repeat the process? I didn't really have enough time with Cassandra."

"No. The drug is much too strong to take more than once. Some of my people have tried to do so, and we really could not pull them back. Are you satisfied now that Cassandra is okay and not in any pain?"

"She's going to be born again on Androvia?"

The alien hesitated. "I... hope so. She has a very strong spirit. You must go now. I have much work to do."

Jack knew the old runaround when he heard it. He didn't trust this alien. Maybe he just wasn't as good a liar as Cassandra.

"Cassandra wanted my sperm and my DNA. What have you done with it?"

The alien didn't answer. He started to reach in his pocket, but Jack was too fast for him. He grabbed his thin arm and pulled out a weapon similar to the one the Draconians had used.

"So, you would kill me rather than answer my questions?"

"Please, you don't understand how important our work is. I know you will not understand what we are doing."

Jack pulled out his own weapon and led the alien back toward the closet where the whining sound was even louder. He pointed his weapon at the closet door.

"I think you have an inter-dimensional transporter in there, just like the Draconian one we destroyed. I'm going to destroy this and leave you stranded here unless I get some answers."

The alien made some squeaking noises and then switched to English. "I... will show you. Please, you will doom our entire race if you destroy the transformer. We do not have the resources to build another before..."

"Before what?"

"Before we die out as a race. I will show you what we are doing, but you will not like it or understand how necessary it is."

203

"Let's take a look at the research you're doing." Jack began walking down the hall.

He passed a bathroom and saw a bedroom. On the other side of the hall was a room that had been set up as a lab. He strode purposely toward a bench where he saw several clear plastic rectangular boxes.

"Stop! You will destroy our work. Your bacteria will contaminate our prototypes."

Jack leaned over for a closer look. It looked like a human-looking fetus. "What the hell are you doing?" he shouted, although part of him already suspected the answer.

The alien reached over to try to restrain Jack, but he pushed him back against the wall. He felt a surge of adrenalin and then red-hot anger. "You're no better than the Draconians. You're experimenting on us. I bet if I have this fetus examined, I'll find that it's half human and half Androvian."

"We are not the same as the Draconians. You don't understand!"

"You don't have much time. Do some explaining or I'll destroy everything here."

The alien was visibly shaking now. He gathered himself and began. "What you see is almost all Androvian. We've only added a very small portion of human DNA. You have something we lack."

"What's that?"

"Look at yourself in the mirror and then look at me. All the biological weapons the Draconians have used on us over time have made us almost infertile. We have few female genotypes that are still viable and are able to reproduce and even fewer men with viable sperm. I'm one of the few male genotypes that have survived, and I lack vitality. Almost all our births are in vitro, but each generation is weaker. It is like a copy of a copy. Soon we no longer will be able to make copies. If we don't introduce a new strain, we will become extinct."

"But you need human DNA to do your experiments, right?"

"Yes...but we do not need to damage humans. We can use small samples from skin, hair, almost any part of a human."

Jack had a horrible thought. "My sperm is part of these specimens, isn't it?"

"We did you no harm," the alien said defensively.

"If you don't want me to destroy these specimens, I expect an honest answer to my next question. I've seen another woman who looked like Cassandra. Do you transport other Androvians here?"

"Our gateway is here. The answer is yes."

"Could a human impregnate one of your women?"

"Not here. We can only do a full in vitro procedure back on Androvia. Here we only can carry a fetus so far and no farther."

Jack thought about the cages where the Draconians held their human experiments and shuddered. He looked more closely at the see-through cubes and saw one contained what looked like a human embryo. He stared at the small face and felt such strong feelings that he had to brace himself against a wall. *Talk about being used, the entire human race and me in particular are being used without our permission,* he thought. "What does all of this mean? You're using my sperm to try to meld our two races' DNA, aren't you? That's what the Draconians are doing. You're no better than them."

Jack stared at the alien who called himself Mark. These aliens were no better than the Draconians. Maybe they were more desperate, but Earth needed to develop without outside interference. Suddenly he knew what he had to do. He headed back toward the living room with the alien close behind him. He reached into his pocket for the alien weapon he had taken from Scarpo, the one he knew was set to kill. He flung open the closet door and saw that most of the space consisted of a large panel with flashing lights and buttons. One corner, though, was bare except for lines that formed a large square. Jack realized that was probably where Androvians stood when coming or going.

"How many of your kind are here right now?"

The alien was shaking even worse now. "You can't do anything to damage this. We cannot establish a new connection from our end. We had to use an abandoned Draconian station the first time, and now it's destroyed."

"How many of your kind are here right now? I don't want to have to ask you again?"

"Just a few. We lost one the other day and we lost Cassandra, so now we are down to myself and two others."

"Why did Cassandra call me *Gliese*?"

The alien hesitated as he stared at the weapon. "You obviously have a Gliesian parent. Their

206

genome is very strong with almost all dominant genetic features."

"Tell me more about the Gliesians!"

"We know very little except that they are a very ancient race that apparently has seeded much of the universe. They appear and disappear; their technology is far advanced from ours. They appear to want to shape the direction different civilizations take."

"Are they allies of the Draconians?"

"No. They are no one's allies."

"How do I contact them?"

"You can't. If they learn about you, I think they will contact you."

"So, I'm a hybrid?"

"You have Gliesian markers in your DNA. You are not completely human, so you already are a hybrid. Look how it has made you stronger and better than most humans. How can you criticize us? You demonstrate that the Gliesians are far ahead of us with their technology. Their genome is much closer to humans and Androvians than to the Draconians as you can tell by how the three races look."

"You never asked any of us for help. You simply took what you needed much like the Draconians. At least they negotiated a treaty with our government, for what that's worth." Jack felt his blood rising.

"You must understand. You prove that humans might help us to survive."

"I don't know what I am or what I prove, but I've sworn allegiance to the human race." Jack headed back toward the living room where the closet door lay closed. The alien tried to grab his arm, but Jack shook him off. He pulled out his weapon and moved the dial all the way to the left the way he had seen Cassandra do.

The alien screamed as the equipment turned to rubble. The whining sound stopped. In the background, Jack heard a dog barking and realized the high frequency weapon probably drove that dog crazy. The alien stared at the rubble in disbelief.

"You've ruined everything. Now we will not survive."

"I've already made sure the Draconians can't return. We humans should determine our own destiny without alien interference."

The alien looked even paler than usual. "You were our last chance, he said.

"Maybe the Gliesians can help you. They seeded your race as well as ours. I'm going to go looking for them now."

"There is little time."

"Then there's even more reason for you to help me contact them. Now here's what I want you to do..." Jack made sure the alien understood the plan and went over some details several times. Finally, the alien nodded that he would cooperate even though he seemed resigned to his race's fate. Jack turned and walked out of the apartment.

Chapter 25

Hawk listened without interrupting while Jack described how he had lost Cassandra. The ex-SEAL tried to control his emotions but soon broke into sobs. He never had allowed himself to show that much emotion when he had been with his team. Now he didn't care about putting on a macho front. Finally he cried himself out and just sat there so exhausted he could barely move, but he knew that he would not be able to sleep.

"You actually saw her? She said that stuff about a different dimension?"

"Yeah, but fat good it does me now. I can't go back and see her even if I die."

Hawk nodded in sympathy but he bubbled with excitement. "I'd love to know what was in that drink the alien gave you."

"It tasted like he wrung out his socks and jock strap. I could barely get it down. Listen, I know how interested you are in all this stuff about different dimensions, but I'm tired of talking about it. All it means to me right now is that I've lost Cassandra forever."

"What do you want to do now?"

"I don't know. I'll probably use the credit card she gave me to pay for a few months in advance and rent a place under my new name. What do you think Scarpo meant when he said I'd never know what Cassandra really was?"

"I don't know. You said she was very human. She bled, so we know she wasn't a robot. You also said you saw someone who looked like her. I don't know if that makes her an android or not. You'd probably have to question that other alien."

"Android? You're much more into the sci-fi stuff than I am. You mean like Commander Data?"

"Kind of except a true android would be built with biological material instead of silicon."

Jack was silent for a few minutes and then shook his head. "She was flesh and blood like us; besides, Mark won't be talking to me anytime soon. I blew up his inter-dimensional transformer. No more trips back and forth to Androvia."

"You blew it up? How could you do that?"

"I took an oath to defend our country, and I'm damned sick of aliens using us like breeding stock. We're entitled to our own destiny without aliens deciding it for us."

"Okay, I'm not the one you should be mad at. I was just thinking we could have learned so much from that machine."

"We'll get there on our own good time schedule, assuming we don't blow ourselves up first. Can I crash at your place tonight?"

"Sure."

Jack reached in his pocket and then reached into a second pants pocket.

"You're probably better off without your cell phone. You know the NSA can track your phone even when it's turned off."

"Great. Any ideas on how I can call home without being tracked? I remember something my father said that was pretty disturbing, and I'm worried about him."

Hawk smiled and motioned for Jack to follow him into his study. He then opened a closet and

210

began digging through piles of electronic equipment. Finally he seemed to find what he was looking for and began connecting several devices together. He then plugged a handset into the pile of electronic junk.

"Use this to call. It bounces your signal all over the place. As far as the NSA can see, this call might just as well be coming from Mars."

Jack thanked him and dialed home since it was past the family's normal dinner hour. The phone rang a few times and then his mother answered.

"Mom?"

"Jack? Where are you? We've had all kinds of people here looking for you."

"It doesn't matter. I'm safe now. Is Dad there?"

"I hoped somehow he was with you." Jack heard his mother's voice break.

"How long has he been missing?"

"He disappeared yesterday, right after coming home from his conference. I heard him arguing with someone over the phone. I usually leave for work before him. When I returned, he was gone. The university said he never showed up for his classes. I don't know what to do!"

"I have an idea. I'll call you when I learn something. He'll be okay. Whoever has him, needs him, so they won't hurt him."

"Jack, be careful. I don't know what I'd do if something happens to both of you. Should I call the police?"

"I don't think they can help; they'll be a lot more interested in finding me than finding Dad. Let me work on it for a couple of days. If I don't find out anything, then you can go to them."

211

"I love you. Please bring your father home safe to me."

"I will." Jack hung up and looked at Hawk. "Someone has kidnapped my father."

"The government?"

"No, I think it has something to do with a crackpot billionaire. Dad gave me a name to call if anything happened to him. I think he realized Anderson might turn violent."

"Can I help?"

"Yeah, I think you can. No one would look for me in the hearse. I'll call this guy, and then we'll pay him a visit."

Jack dialed the number. It rang several times and then a man answered. He spoke in a quivering high-pitched tone.

"Speak!"

"I'm Aaron Starling's son. He gave me this number to call if anything happened to him. I'm supposed to ask for Gerald."

"Are you the SEAL?"

"Yes."

"Maybe we can help. I'll give you directions. Come right away. I don't want to talk about this over the phone. You should know enough about the government to know they can scan for key words."

Gerald gave Jack directions that would require him to drive south and east into a very rural area known as Bonsal. Hawk called the number of an employee who promised he would come and babysit the place in case any bodies arrived. They both got into the front seats of the massive black vehicle and drove toward interstate 5's connection with state route 78.

212

Before very long they were traveling on an empty two-lane highway. The navigation system warned them just in time to make a turn onto a dirt road. Finally they came to a house that was set so far away from the highway that it could not be seen. A dusty jeep was parked in front.

Jack knocked and felt someone watching him although he didn't see a camera.

"Who is that with you?"

"He's my friend. I'll vouch for him."

The door opened and revealed a man with long dark hair with strands of gray fashioned into a ponytail. Dressed in jeans and a white T-shirt, he wore thick black-framed glasses that made his eyes seem even larger as they studied Jack and Hawk.

"Come in. Be quick. I don't want any satellites recording us." The man spoke rapidly and seemed out of breath. His eyes flickered left and right and then repeated the motion.

Gerald led them into a living room filled with books and bookcases. An iMac with a 27-inch screen lay on a desk with a screen saver that displayed the Milky Way. He sat down in a faded green Lazy Boy lounger that had seen better days and motioned for Jack and Hawk to sit across from him.

"Aaron described you to a T."

"How do you know my father? He's never mentioned you."

"Rightly so. He and I went to graduate school together and we've worked on some projects for NASA. Let's say that I'm persona non grata with the agency right now. I've dropped off the grid.

Lately Aaron and I both feared something like this would happen."

"Why would someone kidnap my father?"

"What has he told you?"

"You want me to go first? Okay, I witnessed an argument he had with John Anderson. Mom told me that they argued over the phone just before Dad disappeared. He told me that Anderson's some kind of evangelical crackpot who's liable to do something that could bring the Apocalypse a lot faster. That's all I know."

"Why didn't you go to the police or the government?"

"Let's just say we're not on the best of terms."

Gerald smiled. "Well, then we're all in the same boat. Your father's right about the Apocalypse project, though, and it scares the shit out of me."

"Tell me what you know."

"What do you know about extraterrestrials?"

Jack looked at Hawk before answering. "Earth's kind of neutral territory with aliens from all over the place here legally and illegally including the Draconians. Our government apparently has made an agreement with them."

"Many good people tried to discourage the President from signing that treaty. The military was too excited about the new toys the Draconians promised them, so they talked him into going along. I never trusted those reptiles or their creepy gray henchmen."

"What about my father?"

Gerald began ticking off a laundry list of UFO sightings as well as other evidence of alien activity that he and Jack's father had investigated. He then described the rumors of aliens on the Moon and how they two of them had gone about validating these rumors.

"What about the moon?"

"The astronauts who landed there were warned not to return. If you go through the photos on moonshots, you'll notice many missing ones when it comes to specific sequences of certain locations on the moon. Some of the photos that are available are only available in very low resolution even though the lunar probes' cameras have high definition capability. Ever wonder why?"

"Why?"

Gerald described the conversation that an aging astronaut had with Jack's father in which he revealed to the professor that aliens had warned that the Moon did not belong to humans until they got their affairs in order on Earth and destroyed all nuclear weapons.

"We've chosen to ignore those warnings," Gerald added.

"Who are they and what do they want?"

Gerald shrugged and described a conversation between government agents and a Draconian leader. The reptilian alien told them that the "old ones" mining the Moon were far too powerful even for them. Its advice had been to stay away from them and hope that they continue to ignore Earth.

"What does all of this have to do with Dad?"

Gerald sighed and shook his head. "I guess if you're a billionaire, you can always find someone willing to sell out all our country's secrets regarding the aliens."

"What does it matter? You and Dad know."

215

"It matters if you're John Anderson and you're an evangelical Christian who believes that everything in the *Bible* is the literal word of God. He wants the end of the world to come as quickly as possible so he can wrap himself in his savior's bosom."

"I still don't understand what that has to do with Dad or with the aliens."

"Your father knows a lot about the alien presence on the moon; he's studied them for years as have I. At first Anderson seemed genuinely interested in alien life. Later, it became clear that he wanted to attack the alien base and bring about the end of mankind. He believes the aliens are Lucifer's fallen angels that will bring about the Apocalypse. He knows that the aliens have warned us to stay away from the moon. He thinks that if we attack them, they're bound to retaliate. Hell, if the Draconians are that afraid of those aliens and say that the 'old ones' have weapons far superior to theirs, then what chance does Anderson have of destroying them? Your father told him that the structures on the moon are embedded in the moon's very tough exterior. Nuclear weapons won't destroy them completely."

"Anderson has nuclear weapons?" Jack felt his stomach heave. All it would take is one crazy man with a nuclear attack to destroy everything.

"Sure, with enough money you can buy anything on the open market. He has his command post set up on a private island near some Jamaican resort. He apparently has kidnapped your father because he needs his expertise."

"You seem to have a lot of information. Does the government know what Anderson's planning?"

"There's one bullshit story about Anderson launching a commercial satellite and another one about him launching the first stage of a space elevator for commercial use. He's paid off enough people that no one with any power is looking that closely."

"How do you plan to stop him and save Professor Starling?" Jack said.

Gerald shrugged. "I'm not a SEAL. I have all kinds of logistical info on Anderson's island and on the man himself, but I wouldn't know the first thing about saving him. I suspect your father wanted me to brief you, and figured you could do something to save him."

"Give me everything you have on Anderson and the island," Jack said as he made a decision. He already had begun formulating a plan. He believed he knew where he could get help. *Beauty and the Beast*, he mused to himself.

Chapter 26

Hawk had insisted they watch Casablanca while Jack studied Gerald's files. He shrugged and watched the opening scenes from *Casablanca* flash across the small screen, but soon he was hooked. When it finally ended Hawk said, "Do you understand now why I wanted you to watch this movie?"

"You're saying that our country is kind of like Casablanca but instead of all kinds of spies running around, we have different kinds of aliens; I know that. It's what I told Gerald."

Hawk nodded. "I know, but I wanted you to understand how difficult finding a solution will be. The politics of this whole alien situation are really complicated. The Immigration sign we saw means that more than one kind of alien race probably comes through here. Others like the Androvians bypass the official channels and sneak in. It sounds like any alien race with transporter technology can come and go without detection. That doesn't even account for the "Old Ones" whose home planet apparently is close enough to Earth so that they can use spaceships rather than have to rely on quantum transporters."

"My father was from one of those alien groups, maybe even the 'old ones.' The first time Cassandra saw me, she muttered something about *Gliese*. Later I found out that the Sumerians drew pictures of people who looked like me 5000 years ago and said they were from the stars. There could be other aliens like my father hiding here."

"That's the other thing that bothers me. Anyone from the secret Alien Affairs part of our government will probably recognize you and try to kill you or capture you for dissection."

"I have an idea on how to handle that part of our problem, but I'm going to leave the details to you while I focus on Anderson and my father." Hawk listened while Jack described his plan and then began to jot down a list of what he had to do. He filled one page and began filling a second.

What surprised Jack was that in addition to having information, Gerald also had plenty of money. Despite his small isolated house deliberately located off the grid, he had a wealthy benefactor who believed in learning the truth about the aliens' intentions. Jack revisited a place he thought he never would see again and lined up two members of his assault team. He also drew on alien technology to cover two key parts of his plan.

Saint Benedict's Island is a small speck on the map in the Caribbean. A wealthy Englishman had purchased the land from the British government and later sold it to pay his gambling debts. John Anderson had bought it and then began constructing a huge complex that included an administration building, living quarters, a control center, and a launch pad. The press had accepted his cover story about the construction of a commercial space elevator. Surprisingly, reporters couldn't find any reputable scientists willing to comment on the project. If they had dug more deeply, they would have discovered that many of these scientists had research grants from the Anderson Foundation or one of its many offshoots.

219

Jack marveled at how easy it was to put his plan into operation when money wasn't a problem. He found plenty of people willing sell him what he needed with no questions asked. First class air tickets to Kingston meant expedited boarding and express luggage service once the plane landed.

Jack had chosen a moonless night for his operation. He and his crew of two identical looking women dragged the compact rubber boat up through the sand and hid it behind some rocks. The women moved gracefully and silently although each of them carried a full backpack loaded with equipment.

I sure hope this works; otherwise, we'll have to use force, Jack thought. Each of them carried Androvian weapons far superior to the Carl Gustav Ricky had provided on their battle with the Draconians. Jack also carried communications equipment as well as a small device upon which the entire operation would depend. If the alien who called himself Mark had wanted to avenge the destruction of his quantum transporter by destroying him, now would be his perfect opportunity.

Jack took out a penlight and studied the space center's plans. It was late enough that Anderson would likely be in his master bedroom. He directed the device and aimed the narrow band antenna in the right direction. He had a microphone as well as recordings Hawk had made in his sonorous deep voice. The device's screen displayed the complex's architectural plans and a small blinking light moved until it was centered in the section labeled *Master Bedroom*. He flipped a switch and he saw the room

220

displayed with an infrared image of a kneeling figure.

Jack pressed a button and began transmitting.

The monitor along with the whispered words made it clear that John Anderson was praying.

"Lord, I long for the Rapture so I can be one with you. Let me be your instrument!"

Jack pressed another button, and an illuminated object began to take form in the darkened room. Majestic and clad in traditional robes, the stately figure of Jesus began speaking.

Jack pressed a button and Hawk's sonorous voice beamed into Anderson's bedroom once more.

"You will be my sword that I might slay the Evil One."

"Yes, Lord."

"You have proof of Lucifer's handiwork, my child?"

"I have photos and reports from NASA. I even have the only copy of an agreement Truman signed with the fallen angels."

"You have done well, my child, but the real work has not yet begun. Are you strong enough in body and spirit?"

"Let me strike the first blow, Lord."

"You are my loyal servant, and I will honor you in the next world for your brave efforts."

Anderson spoke softly. "Lord, I am your humble servant. Tell me what to do."

Jesus paused for a moment before speaking and then continued. "I have plans for Aaron Starling. You must release him immediately and send him to the beach without anyone nearby; they would not be able to see what happens to him and live. Your men must not hurt him."

"Yes, Lord. I will do your bidding!" Jack smiled when he heard those words.

"I know you plan to launch your weapon very soon. Lucifer is starting to muster his fallen angels. I want you to speed up your launch to 10 am this morning. That will still give your scientists time to do their recalculations."

"It will be done."

Jack stared through binoculars and saw his father coming out of the building. Lights were going on throughout the facility. Professor Starling walked by himself toward the beach. Security guards were nowhere in sight. Jack rose and beckoned for his father to come closer. One of the women with Jack led the professor to the dingy and rowed it toward a larger boat that was moored just beyond the horizon.

Jack and his accomplice stood behind a rocky outgrowth. There had been plenty of activity at the launch site. She pointed an object at the rocket and pressed several buttons until she seemed satisfied and then nodded to Jack.

At precisely 10 am, the huge rocket's engines bellowed a deafening sound and flames pushed it up into the sky. Jack watched the rocket's trail and crossed his fingers. As he followed the rocket's path, he noticed it was starting to turn much too soon in flight. It continued to turn and then dipped as it headed down toward the ocean. It then seemed to accelerate before it hit the water and created a huge wave.

Jack and the woman waited until dark and then the dingy returned for them. The boat took them to Kingston and where they caught a flight back to the United States. Their flight plan included a three-hour layover at JFK in order to catch a direct flight back to San Diego.

The TV monitor mounted across from Jack and the two women displayed an old *Law and Order* episode. Jack glanced up and saw that the actors had been replaced with the face of a very agitated reporter who was talking very fast. A map behind the reporter displayed an area in the Caribbean near Jamaica. Jack stood and moved closer to read the text crawling across the bottom of the screen.

"I don't believe it," Jack muttered to himself as he read the words flashing across the screen. The island where billionaire John Anderson had failed to successfully launch the world's first commercial space platform had just been destroyed by what appeared to be a meteor storm. The firestorm destroyed the Space Development Corporation's facility along with all employees. Billionaire John Anderson was reportedly among the dead.

We got Dad out just in time, Jack thought. He had a sudden thought, but it struck him as too wild to be possible. Was the firestorm an act of nature, or alien retribution?

Chapter 27

"Thank God for Arizona and its carry law," Jack said as he eyed the group of heavily tattooed men carrying weapons. Ricky smiled at him and waved.

"My kind of state," he said.

Jack had rented the grand ballroom of the largest hotel in Phoenix for the occasion. Hawk had been busy for several days making the arrangements. He had set up websites all over the world under several aliases so that they could not easily be shut down quickly. He also had arranged FTP sites in a number of countries. His handouts would include the website addresses.

"This makes Wiki Leaks look like a drop in the bucket," Hawk said proudly.

Gerald and a number of his friends had been an active part of the plan. Professor Starling had lined up several key scientists who had flown in for the event. He had squirreled away his blockbuster secret guests in an adjacent room backstage.

Professor Starling and several of his scientist colleagues had cashed in all the favors various media personalities owed them. Jack looked around and saw signs on cameras that identified all three major networks as well as all the major cable networks. He smiled when he saw that chance had stationed MSNBC and FOX adjacent to each other. Then again, maybe that had been Hawk's idea of a joke.

Hawk put an arm around Jack's and pointed to a section of chairs that had been reserved for print media. He pointed to the *New York Times* science reporter as well as a famous science writer who had joined *Yahoo News*. *The Los Angeles Times'* seat was between seats reserved for reporters from the *Washington Post* and *USA Today*.

Jack saw a figure motioning him over with a wave of her hand. "That's Sally Thompson from the Associated Press," Hawk whispered. They walked over to where she sat.

"You gentlemen promised something of 'earthshaking significance.' I hope you can deliver. I have a deadline in two hours."

"You won't be disappointed," Hawk assured her. He led Jack back to the stage.

"It's been like this all morning. There are a million things that might go wrong. What if the government sends goons to break up the press conference?"

"They'll have to shoot their way past Ricky and his gang. I know they're just itching for a chance to make the evening news. If worse comes to worse, I'll shoot the Draconian weapon and make everyone fall flat on their face."

"How come it didn't make you sick? I've been wondering that ever since our trip to New Mexico."

Jack smiled weakly. He had wondered that as well. He thought he might know the answer, but he didn't really want to believe it. "I guess it's just good conditioning."

Jack saw his mother talking to someone who looked like another lawyer. Marjorie Starling had been her usual meticulous self once she had learned what would take place; she had assigned her law firm's staff to work with the press as well as to serve as a barrier to government inquiries. NASA had become curious when it saw so many astrophysicists listed in the initial press release, but the Starling law firm had replied in very vague legalese and refused to be specific.

Professor Starling stood on the stage and looked at the audience. He saw several men in dark suits who appeared to have wireless microphones and ear buds. His normally placid face flushed as he motioned Jack to his side.

"Do you see those clowns in their dark suits and ties talking into those earpieces? They can't hide who they are. I've been fighting those nameless, faceless government bureaucrats my entire life. I wouldn't be surprised if one of their goon squads killed Frank Buchanan."

"It's time to start, Dad. Give them hell!" Jack said and handed him the microphone before walking off the stage. Professor Starling introduced himself and then began his presentation.

"This press conference is being streamed throughout the world and you will find in the press packs being passed out a list of websites located in several countries where you will be able to download support materials that provide undeniable proof of what we will present today."

Professor Starling signaled and lights dimmed as his presentation appeared on a large screen behind him. The first slide showed a couple of NASA's recent photos of the Moon.

"The slide on the left is the one currently present on NASA's website; you'll note the low resolution that makes it impossible to see concrete details. Of course NASA also has some high-resolution pictures that it failed to include on its

226

website. The picture on the right is a photo of the exact same moon location, but this time it is the high-resolution version that has been provided to me without NASA's knowledge or approval. You'll note the vague shadows in the first picture now reveal the presence of definite structures as well as the outline of an enormous spaceship."

The room broke into bedlam. Starling called on the CBS reporter.

"Professor Starling, what proof do we have that you haven't used a photo editing program to create this image, especially if NASA denies that this second photo is legitimate?"

Jack had anticipated this question, and the team had prepared a strategy for every question they could imagine.

"I will provide you with statements from people who have worked with NASA that will authenticate this photo along with the statement and video recording of an astronaut."

The audience exploded with several reporters shouting and demanded that their questions be addressed. Instead, he motioned his son to the platform and introduced him before handing him the microphone.

Jack heard some people in the audience groan. One man whispered, "We came all this way to listen to some nutcases?" Jack pointed to an NBC reporter.

"Isn't it true that you have been treated recently for mental problems?"

"I've been treated for PTSD as a result of my military experience in Afghanistan. You can decide whether or not I'm sane after I introduce some people to you and demonstrate some things."

Jack watched as four men dragged a large lead block onto the stage. He asked two male reporters in the front row to climb onto the stage and verify that the block on display was solid and very heavy. The two men strained to move it and then nodded to the audience before taking their seats.

Jack took the small Draconian weapon out of his pocket. "You'll note that the barrel is solid with no opening. This is a weapon I confiscated from an extraterrestrial, a member of a group that resides here on Earth because of a treaty our government has signed with them."

Once again voices in the audience rose until it was difficult to hear anyone speak. Jack pointed his weapon at the lead block and pressed the button. The lead block exploded. Jack then dialed the weapon to the right and pointed it at the audience. He fired as they gasped. The audience lay prone for several minutes and then started to recover.

"This is a high frequency weapon that can kill, but it also can be used to disable humans as you now realize."

Jack showed a picture of a Draconian in disguise and then one in its natural state as the audience gasped. He then pointed to the screen that now displayed what looked like a legal document.

"This is a copy of the treaty signed by President Truman that gave the Draconians access to our precious metals as well as permission to perform experiments on humans in exchange for their technology."

"This is ridiculous," a reporter from a cable network shouted. "We've heard these lies for decades now!"

"All the support material we're providing will back up my statements. I now would like to introduce you to some aliens from a world known as Androvia."

The audience stared at the door behind the stage when it opened and two identical women along with the male Androvian called Mark strode to where Jack stood.

"How do we know they're aliens?" a reporter shouted.

Jack nodded and a man sitting in front row came onto the stage. Jack handed him the microphone.

"I'm Professor Franklin Jamison of the University of California at San Diego Medical School. I have a degree from Harvard Medical School and served my fellowship in genetics at Yale Medical School. I have taken blood samples from these two females as well as the male and can verify that their DNA is distinctly not human. I repeated the tests several times."

Several reporters shouted their questions, but the researcher handed the microphone back to Jack who said, "All of Professor Jamison's results are available online. Now, I have something to say that you might find even more unbelievable, but once again, Professor Jamison has verified the results which are available online."

Jack faced the audience and found the words difficult to say, but he forced himself. "I am the product of a human female and a male from a race known as the Gliesians. They all tend to look very much like me. The Androvians I have introduced require the help of this race to preserve their own. Now that everything is out in the open, I'm asking for any extraterrestrials known as the Gliesians to contact me so they can help the Androvian race survive. They need help immediately."

Jack gestured toward the projection booth. The lights dimmed and Frank Buchanan's face filled the screen. The audience gasped as they recognized the iconic figure. The astronaut's familiar voice filled the room as he began describing fifty years of lies and deception by a government that feared its citizens would not be able to handle the truth about the presence of extraterrestrials. When Buchanan finished speaking and the lights went on again, Jack turned his microphone back to his father.

Professor Starling had tears in his eyes after watching his old friend's last words. "I have supporting documents from Major Buchanan including copies of memoranda written by a clandestine group known as Majestic-12. All of these materials are available on the various websites listed. Many of these website are located in neutral countries where our government has no power to shut them down."

"All the details are online, including pictures that NASA has deleted from its website. You'll see how each of her spaceflights have been monitored and closely followed by alien spacecraft. You'll also find signed letters from several astronauts that confirm this information. It's much too late for our government to continue to lie to us and to the rest of the world."

230

"Documents will prove that there is an alien immigration center under the Denver Airport. A file on our websites will provide architectural proof. Our government has been actively admitting some alien races while refusing to admit others. That must stop as well as its support for this evil race known as the Draconians. Now, I'm going to turn the microphone over to several internationally known scientists to come up to the stage to offer concrete proof that the moon is being mined by aliens." Jack listened as his father and his colleagues went through several slides. Like professors all over the world, though, they were a bit too long-winded. Meanwhile, Ricky and his security group were menacing enough to prevent anyone from storming the stage.

As Professor Starling was concluding, a rear door opened and a police officer with a bullhorn shouted, "This meeting is illegal. We are asking you to end it right now."

The audience erupted in righteous indignation. Ricky's group simply glared at the officer and raised their weapons. The officer backed off.

Hawk sat down next to Jack and whispered, "I'm getting word that the NSA or some other government agency is trying to block our websites, but they can't. I have websites in Switzerland, Russia, and other countries that don't really care what our government wants. I've also managed to download files to international media as well as our major media. It's too late now to stop people from reading the facts!"

Hawk stopped talking and picked up his phone and listened intently before smiling. "Fox News has suspended its programming to cover this event. The *New York Times* is sending out news flashes as well. It doesn't matter what the government tries to do to us now because the word is finally out."

Jack nodded. His father sat down next to him while a colleague answered questions from the audience about structures on the moon.

"Does this mean I don't get my fellowship?" Jack asked with a smile.

"I'm afraid so, but I've waited all my life to see this information made public." After the meeting ended, Jack and his father spent another two hours being interviewed. From the corner of his eye, he saw that Mark and the alien women were big hits, particularly for the television reporters.

As the media began digesting the material on the various websites, the government remained silent. Jack realized, *they probably don't know how to react. Do they admit they've been lying all these years or do they stonewall? Sending the files to members of the opposition party in Congress had been Hawk's brilliant idea.*

"Will they arrest us when we try to leave?" Professor Starling asked his son.

"I've talked with Mom about it. She's called in some favors from pretty high-powered lawyers. They've already announced that we acted in the public's interest and that they would resist any attempts to arrest or prosecute us."

Jack saw his mother approaching him while she talked on her cell phone. She had a grim look on her face. She hung up and faced the two men in her life.

"It looks like they're going to play hardball with us. The Attorney General is claiming we will be prosecuted for revealing top-secret documents. I have friends close to our current President as well as his predecessor. I wouldn't be surprised to find that they knew very little about all this. I think they might plead ignorance and go after some of the NSA people instead of us."

"Will they arrest us as we try to leave?" Professor Starling said.

"I honestly don't know. I've already responded that my office is legal counsel and that we take full responsibility that you both will report for any hearing. I've made that note public and sent it to all the major media. My hope is that arresting you right now will look bad in the public's eyes."

Marjorie Starling gave one hand to our husband and the other to her son and led them through the hall's rear doors. There was bedlam outside. Police were trying to keep a mob away from the building. A group stood with signs proclaiming, "Thanks for Telling the Truth" and "Shame on Our Government!"

Marjorie spoke briefly to a distinguished looking man and then nodded. "You're in my custody and I've promised you will report as ordered; meanwhile, we'll call in the big legal guns. I think every civil rights and free speech attorney looking to make a name for himself is going to offer free representation."

Jack went home to his parents' home. There was no reason to do otherwise. He had gratefully accepted Ricky's offer to provide security. His friend was enjoying the spotlight. No goons would grab them in the middle of the night without facing several men who were hungering for a chance to use some pretty potent weapons. Jack had a few of the Draconian weapons on hand if worse came to worse.

Professor Starling opened his PC and began scanning the web. He hummed a tune to himself. "Do you see what the *Los Angeles Times* is saying? Their editorial is saying that we're heroes. The *New York Times* is demanding we be absolved of any prosecution because we served the country well by revealing this dirty secret that the public had the right to know."

"We'll see how supportive everyone will be when they start threatening to throw us in solitary for twenty years."

"Don't even say it." The usually-reserved Marjorie Starling was close to tears.

Professor Starling paced the floor. "Look at what the Speaker of the House is saying. He's demanding a full investigation of how the administration has hidden the truth from the American people."

"What about the President's own party?" Marjorie said.

Starling scanned his monitor for a few minutes before responding. "It looks like the tide is turning in our favor. The Majority Leader is demanding answers as well. The senior Senator from California says we're heroes."

Chapter 28

Marjorie Starling described to Jack how shocked she had been to receive the call. She listened to the caller and then raised her hand to signal her receptionist not to interrupt her. She checked her conference room schedule and provided a range of dates and times. She then reserved the room and immediately called her son.

Jack was trying to avoid the press as well as any government goons looking for him by staying with Hawk. His friend frowned when he heard the news.

"It could be a trap. If they know where you'll be and when you'll be there, it will be easy enough to grab you."

"I have to do this," Jack said.

He took the Coaster public transportation downtown; his car would be too noticeable as well as to easy to follow. He entered the building adjacent to the one housing his mother's law firm via a basement parking garage and then found a fourth-floor connecting bridge; he avoided the elevator and took the stairs to reach the law office. As he entered the office, his mother's administrative assistant motioned for him to go directly into the firm's conference room.

The carpeting was deep and luxurious as were the cushioned chairs while the lack of glass windows or doors ensured complete privacy. He closed the door and then saw a large figure seated in the far corner. As he drew closer, the figure pointed to a chair across from him.

"It's like looking in a mirror," Jack said.

"Our unique genotype is a blessing and a curse, depending on the situation." The man spoke with a slight accent, but nothing that identified him as a resident of a particular region or country.

"You're my father?"

"I assume so. I have contacted your biological mother who confirmed what I suspected when I saw you on television."

"I don't understand exactly what you were doing here?"

"You mean here on Earth?"

"Yeah."

He sighed and didn't speak for a couple of minutes and then shrugged in a very human gesture. "I'm not really sure how to answer that question. Nothing is really that simple. Quite frankly, I'm very surprised to be having this conversation."

"You knew you had fathered me?"

"No, I am not so different from you that I don't have feelings. I cared very much for your mother; I never thought that she could conceive since we're not an exact match as far as our DNA."

"But if you cared so much, how could you just leave her without a word, without even saying goodbye?"

"By staying with her, I was putting her life in danger as well as my own and my mission. It's difficult to explain to you how complex the situation was and is, but I'm sure as a SEAL you understand the importance of completing your mission."

"Who would hurt you?"

"You mean besides your own government? I suppose the list would include every other government capable of spying as well as several alien entities that I'm sure you never knew existed."

"The Draconians?"

"Of course I'd put them high on my list, but the Lyrians, the Androvians, and the Travelers all had good reason to fear my kind enough to kill me. Your crazy billionaire with his nuclear toys would have tried as well."

"You're what the Androvians call the 'old ones,' aren't you?"

"Does it really matter what they call us? They all want what we have achieved over the centuries."

"The Androvians want to use your DNA to create hybrids so they can survive as a race. Is that such a terrible thing?"

The man smiled, but it was more of a grimace. "You obviously became very attached to one of them, didn't you?"

Jack nodded. "We had made plans to be together, but a Draconian killed her. I saw her after her death, but she told me I didn't belong there."

It was the other man's turn to show genuine surprise now. "You took the Filian potion and survived? I didn't think it was possible for your kind."

"Well, I did. Why can't you help them? They're asking so little of you?"

The man's voice grew louder and he showed genuine emotion now. "So little? I understand you destroyed their quantum transporter because they were using you for the very same thing you believe I should give them freely."

"I didn't know they were using me. You would be doing it intentionally at their request."

"It would make little difference. They are far less human than your people are. They aspire to be human, but they lack your race's emotional capabilities, and they never will achieve that."

Now it was Jack's turn to be angry. "That's not true! Cassandra cared about me. I know she did."

"She must have read up on human emotions; the Androvians are quick studies. Did you ever see her cry or laugh with genuine emotion?"

Jack thought hard, but he couldn't remember. He knew Cassandra had to have shown real emotion, she couldn't be what her father suggested. Was he absolutely positive she hadn't faked her organisms?

"I remember her showing genuine emotion; I would have known if she were faking."

The older man smiled, but it was a sad smile. "You humans place such a premium on that. Maybe you would be better off as a race if your females' behinds turned red when they were in heat. At least then you'd recognize genuine passion."

Jack started to object, but his father raised his hand and motioned for him to hold what he wanted to say. "I understand you were responsible in part for the destruction of the missile aimed at your Moon. Is that true?"

"Yes, I didn't want one crazy person to bring about the end of the world."

"His weapon would not have detonated with our force fields in place, but you didn't know that. It is true we might have overreacted, so you did the right thing. We made sure that problem would never reoccur. We also sent a not so subtle message to your government. I also learned that you also have

238

destroyed the Draconians' transporter; you've been a very busy boy."

"You disapprove of what I did?"

The alien shook his head slowly and thoughtfully. "No, but you were being used by the Androvians. It is important to know when you are being used, and it is not always an easy thing. Why do you think your government sided with the Draconians and not with the Androvians?"

The question stunned Jack because the answer seemed so obvious. "Because the Draconians only destroy. They have no culture and they plan to take over the Earth."

He shook his head slowly. "That's what the Androvians told you, and I suppose it makes perfect sense if you only hear one side of the story. We have a saying that there are three sides to every argument."

"Are you saying the Androvians are evil and the reptiles are good? I don't believe that! I saw what they did to my buddy and to others. They were experimenting on them."

"Why do you think they were experimenting on them?" The alien sounded like a patient teacher quizzing a very slow student.

"Because they want to create a hybrid race that can live on this planet."

"You sound so sure of yourself. It is true that the Draconians are brutal and primitive in many ways. They certainly are not an attractive race, but they play a role in the grand scheme of things. You are aware that your planet's climate is changing, are you not?"

239

"Sure, I assume when the air's too poisoned for us, the Draconians will come to the surface and live here."

The Gliesian's laugh was short and unpleasant. "Those poor creatures cannot breed on this planet nor can they survive long because of their bulk and your planet's gravity. Part of their arrangement with your government was to help develop a hybrid race that could survive the climate conditions your race's stupidity are creating."

"I don't believe you. What do they get out of it?"

"Well, nothing much now that you have destroyed their ability to transport valuable minerals back to their world. They have little excuse now to cooperate and may turn even more violent."

"Then you should help the Androvians since they have technology that can contain the Draconians."

The alien dismissed that statement with a hand gesture. "None of these races pose a threat to this world as long as we decide they should not. We have the power to destroy all of them, and they know it."

"So, what gives your people the right to play God and decide which races live and which ones die?"

"Interesting question. We seeded this world and most of the others including the worlds of the Draconians, the Lyrians, the Travelers, and your friends, the Androvians. So, in effect, we have been God to all these races. Does that answer your question?"

"When I destroyed the transporters, I did so because humans should control their own destinies and not have to grovel to alien races to beg for survival."

"Interesting choice of words, but I understand you are a warrior. No one is asking humans to grovel. They simply are not ready for venturing beyond this world until they are willing to give up their nuclear weapons. They cannot be allowed to threaten other worlds that are occupied by other intelligences."

"So you make the rules for everyone?"

His biological father shook his head sadly. "We all are controlled by powers beyond our own. We also die and go to a place we did not create. Still, our civilization is so much older than the others around us, we feel an obligation to ensure that all intelligent entities survive and do not kill each other off. We do not want to be alone in this vast universe."

"What do you want from me?"

"I guess I had a very human impulse to want to see my biological son after I found out you exist. I also understand that you presently are not employed, is that true?"

"Yes, who would hire me? Half the people avoid me because they think I'm insane while the other half fear me. After all, I told the world that I'm half-alien."

"You are unique, and apparently you held your own with the Androvians and Draconians who both are known as very efficient killers. We think you could play a very valuable role now that the Moon's secrets have been exposed."

241

"I won't spy for your people."

"You don't understand. We have been in contact with your government and they agree that you would make the ideal bridge between our races. We already have made it clear to your Majestic-12 group through some extreme measures we have taken that should they try to harm you, we will intervene in a very unpleasant way. The result of our conversation with this group is that they now find you acceptable as the first Ambassador to our people. What you learn from us, you then can bring back here to Earth."

"Doesn't that mean that you just want to use me just as you say the Draconians and the Androvians tried to use me? You'll try to brainwash me to become a defender of everything your race does."

The older man looked thoughtful and bit his lip before replying. "In exchange for helping your people see the need to destroy their nuclear weapons, we are prepared to give you the stars. You'll be able to explore the universe and even colonize any uninhabited planets you find. It would mean that your race never must fear that a collision with a meteor might mean the end of your kind. You will spread through the universe and make your homes on countless planets."

Jack's eyes brightened as he thought of that possible future. "What if a country believes America is just trying to disarm them to conquer them?"

"We believe you can convince them of the error of their ways with our help, of course."

Jack saw a bottle of Scotch and some glasses on a sideboard. He rose and filled two glasses and then gave one to the biological father he had never known.

"Let's toast the future of humanity on a hundred different worlds," he said.

THE END